THEIRS TO TAKE

NATASHA KNIGHT

Copyright © 2015 by Natasha Knight

All rights reserved.

No part of this book may be reproduced in any form or by any electronic or mechanical means, including information storage and retrieval systems, without written permission from the author, except for the use of brief quotations in a book review.

❦ Created with Vellum

PROLOGUE

"No, not that one."

I had never felt so relieved to hear Syn's voice or feel his cane at my thigh as I did in that moment.

"That one isn't for sale," he spoke quietly, his tone low, but there was no question he would be obeyed.

I turned to meet his dark gaze. The grin that curled one corner of his mouth upward sent ice through my veins. He kept his black eyes on mine as he tapped the cane against the fronts of my thighs once, twice, then with a flick of his wrist, lashed me with it.

Tears stung my eyes nearly as badly as the rattan did my legs and I took a step backward, looking down at the welt rising where he'd struck, grateful that the man who had been considering me nodded with a reluctant growl before stepping to my right, to the next girl who stood shuddering beside me.

Gabriel, Syn's brother, joined him. Both kept their eyes on me as Gabriel whispered something into Syn's ear. Syn nodded, then turned his attention from me to the girl who was being handled now. Gabriel, the older, more stern of the two, approached me. My gaze faltered and my body shook but I refused to look away.

"Evangeline," he said, calling my name. "Kneel."

Once a girl was sold, she was made to kneel so that the next buyers knew who was still available. The girl beside me whimpered and I turned to see the large man weighing her breasts, turning her nipples in his fingers.

"I'd like to try her," he said, his voice gruff.

Syn's eyebrow went up. The girl stood upright, naked, her hands clasped at the back of her head. He looked her over, his gaze cold even as the girl now openly wept.

Syn turned back to the man. "You can look. You can even touch," he said, turning the girl so she stood with her back to the man. He then pushed her forward, forcing her to bend deeply at the waist. "But you can't *fuck* until you pay."

"Evangeline." Gabriel's grip in my hair demanded my full attention so I could only listen to the girl's whimpers as he brought his mouth to my ear. "I said kneel. Eyes down. And just be glad it isn't you this time."

Without giving me time to obey, he forced me down by my hair until I knelt. I stared up at him, but my defiance lasted only a moment when I saw the darkness in those beautiful, golden eyes. I cast my gaze to the ground before me, swallowing, shivering at what was to be my fate if the brothers truly kept me as I knew now they would.

1

The drive had taken me more than an hour out of the city and I now stood in heels and an evening gown, shivering behind the heavy support of a bridge, trying to keep out of sight. It was too late to turn back. They'd hear my four-inch heels clicking if I ran, but after what I'd seen, all I wanted to do was flee. When I'd followed him here, I hadn't been sure what I'd expected to find, but it certainly wasn't *this*.

"Where's Jamison?" Arthur, my fiancé, snapped. I'd only recently become familiar with that harsh tone. He still wore the tux he'd had on at the fundraiser earlier this evening and looked at odds with the men who surrounded him.

"On his way. Had some trouble with one of the girls."

I didn't recognize the man who spoke, but I vaguely knew the one they referred to: Jamison. He worked for Arthur. I'd seen Jamison a few times, always in the background, never introduced, but always there, always watching.

"You're not using enough of the sedative. How many times do I have to tell you that?" Arthur barked.

As I watched, he walked around to where two other men opened the back of a large livestock truck, which was parked not too far away, lined up neatly with several others.

"Let's get them loaded and ready." Arthur checked his watch. "Shipment's got to move fast."

The two men moved to a van standing nearby with its engine still running. When they opened the door and I saw what was inside, I gasped. I covered my mouth, hoping the rumbling of the engine would mask the sound. Arthur looked in my direction, but I hid behind the wide support, holding my breath.

"Let's go," he said.

I peered back around to watch as Arthur, a man I'd known for just over a year, the man with whom I lived, whom I thought I loved, hauled an unconscious woman over his shoulder and carried her to the waiting truck. There, one of the men took her, wrapped something around her wrist and handed her up to yet another man who stood waiting inside the truck. They did the same with a second woman, but they weren't done yet. I watched, stunned and terrified as the men loaded four more women up into the same truck.

I was so engrossed with what was happening that I didn't hear the sound of another vehicle approach, not until I stood flooded in its headlights. I turned to it, too shocked to move until it came to a stop, the front passenger door opening, a man running toward me. Suddenly animated, I screamed and ran, nothing but the clacking sounds of my heels in the dark night, followed too closely by the heavier footfalls of the men now pursuing me.

Someone tackled me, sending me sprawling onto the gravel road, pain shooting through my knees, the heels of my hands, my face as I hit the ground hard, the weight of the man on my back keeping me pinned. The fall knocked the wind out of me, leaving me gasping, and I'd never forget the smell of the man who held me down, his breath hot on the side of my face.

"What the hell?" Arthur called out. He too had been chasing me, for when the man who had tackled me hauled me to my feet, I met Arthur's hard gaze, the tears in my eyes blurring his image.

His surprised expression gave way to fierce anger, a rage I'd never before seen.

"Arthur?" My voice trembled and my stomach sank.

He looked at me, then at Jamison who now stood beside him, still dressed in the tuxedo he'd worn to tonight's dinner. Jamison shook his head and reached into his pocket, retrieving a syringe and handing it to Arthur. When Arthur approached, I tried to take a step back, but the hands that held me only tightened around my arms.

"Arthur?" I asked again, terror gripping me at what I saw in his eyes.

"You should have stayed at the hotel like I told you, Eva." He clutched a handful of my hair and painfully turned my head, making me cry out. "But you never were any good at doing what you were told, were you?"

"Stop, please!"

The tip of the needle stabbed into my neck, the pain instantaneous as he depressed the plunger and emptied the contents into me.

"Arthur—"

The men released me as he pulled the needle out. I stumbled forward, everything blurring. I reached out to steady myself, my hands sliding off Arthur's chest, too weak to hold on. Arthur's grip in my hair tightened and I took a step as he moved me, but that was my final step, because my legs failed me then. He had to drag me after that, muttering something under his breath. I managed to call out to him one more time, looking up at him just before he slammed my head against the side of the truck. Pain exploded behind my eyes, blinding me, and I slid down onto the grime-covered gravel, my fingers closing around the toe of his shoe. He pulled it away, then, with his foot, rolled me onto my belly. His hand wrapped around my wrist, pulling my arm up at a painful angle while fingers tugged at my engagement ring, sliding it off my finger before he barked his next command.

"Get her loaded with the rest of them.

※

"There's something special in tonight's shipment."

Gabriel listened to the informant's message. It was brief and to the point, but still vague enough if anyone had somehow managed to tap the line. He turned to Syn who stood looking over their selection of firearms.

His little brother liked their job entirely too much.

"You about ready?" Gabriel asked, sliding the phone into his pocket.

"What do you think?" Syn asked. "Can't decide between American made or German."

Gabriel picked up his preferred pistol, a lightweight weapon he knew well. "When in doubt, go American, brother. Always." He checked his watch. "And hurry up or we'll miss the rendezvous point."

"Rendezvous," Syn said, chuckling. "You're funny. You mean ambush."

"Call it whatever you want to call it, but move your ass.

There are a dozen girls in this shipment and I just got word one is special."

Syn picked up the American made machine gun. "Special, huh?"

They walked up the stairs and out the door to the pickup truck.

"He didn't elaborate but he's never let us down. Let's go."

"Take it easy," Syn said, climbing into the passenger seat as Gabriel started the engine. "We haven't missed a *rendezvous* yet. Curious about what's special though."

"Me too."

They drove down the winding road of their property, the automatic gates opening as they neared. They then left the large, gothic style mansion behind.

2

My head throbbed like someone had hit it with a baseball bat. I moaned, unable to feel anything but pain, unable even to open my eyes.

"But sir, she's..." someone argued.

"I said get her loaded." It was Arthur voice.

"Sir," it sounded like Jamison, his voice hushed. "Moving the timeline up?"

"Just make sure there's only twelve left on that truck at the drop off point. You know what you have to do. No fuck ups, nothing linking back to me. Otherwise, make it look good. And alert me as soon as the others have been dropped."

"Yes, sir," came Jamison's voice as arms hauled me upward, lifting me off the ground only to drop me onto a hard, cold surface, an awful stench all around me. I tried to speak, but nothing came, it was as though I was unable to make my mouth move. I tried to touch the throbbing spot on my head, but couldn't lift my arm. Couldn't make my limbs move. I felt myself slipping in and out of consciousness, hearing men talking around me. A gloved hand took hold of mine and a heavy chain was wrapped around my wrist.

"It fucking stinks in there," someone said. He must have jumped off the truck because I heard the sound of boots crunching gravel followed by a grunt.

He was right — it did stink. It stank of a barn.

A loud bang signaled the closing of a door, the grate of metal on metal as the lock slid into place. Then the engine roared to life, the smell of exhaust filling my lungs. The tires of the truck rumbled beneath me, my body bouncing with each bump in the road.

All I wanted to do was sleep. My head hurt, my mind was foggy, and I felt like I was moving through mud as I tried to bring my arm to my face. I gave myself over to it, not having the strength to fight. Someone lifted my head and laid it on something soft and warm, and finally, I slept.

࿐

THE ANGRY BLARE OF A CAR HORN WOKE ME AND I COULD HEAR the sound of quiet weeping. I wasn't alone. The soft pillow beneath me shifted and I realized my head was cradled on someone's lap. I tried to open my eyes but something covered them. The smell was awful, and I remembered I'd been loaded onto a truck. I reached to my face and pushed the blindfold off my eyes, blinking several times to clear my vision. It was nighttime, the passing glow of streetlights illuminating the gloomy interior of the truck's enclosure.

The dim light confirmed the source of the stench — we were on a livestock truck. We were being transported like cattle.

Blinking through the pain of a throbbing headache, I hauled myself upright and scanned the row of occupants in the truck. A bump in the road had us all bouncing and several of the women screamed. I looked at them, at the dozen or so women in the truck with me. We were all chained together in pairs, some sleeping while others peered around with wide, frightened eyes.

The woman I was bound to pulled her arm up to scratch her face, tugging at the chain that linked us. "You okay?" she asked, her voice a whisper.

She was the one who had laid my head on her lap.

I sat upright and leaned against the wall of the truck to look at her. She seemed to be around my age, in her early twenties — all of the women did — and they were all attractive, all in various states of dress.

My memory was foggy. I looked down at myself. I still wore the dress I'd had on for the fundraiser, but it was torn in several places and filthy. A chill made me shiver and I hugged my knees up against my chest, trying to remember, trying to figure out what had happened. The last thing I remembered was Arthur wanting to have one more drink when we'd gotten back to the hotel from the fundraiser. He had looked anxious, and Jamison, his personal bodyguard, had been nearby. Arthur had wanted to get rid of me, I remembered that much. He had told me to go to bed. That he'd come up soon.

But I hadn't gone to bed. I'd followed him somewhere. But where?

I squeezed my eyes shut and forced myself to take a long, deep breath in, exhale, and repeat, before turning to the girl next to me. Her brown eyes were wide, frightened. "What's happening? Where are we?"

"I don't know. I was at a nightclub and this guy bought me a drink. We were talking for a while, then I felt strange and… that's all I remember."

"Me too," another girl said from the other side of the truck.

The girl next to me began to cry quietly and I took her hand, holding it tightly. I looked at my companions, their frightened eyes reflecting the glow of passing streetlights. Streetlights that seemed to be less and less frequent. I lifted my bound arm to see if I could loosen the chain, but it was thick and heavy. Impossible. And even if I could remove it, there was no way off of the moving truck.

Was Arthur back at the hotel now? Would he know I was missing?

The throbbing of my head put an end to that thought and I couldn't shake the feeling of dread.

I touched my thumb to the engagement ring he'd given me half a year ago right when we'd bought our house together, but a new panic overcame me. Raising my hand, I looked at my finger, at the tan line there where a ring should have been.

It was gone.

Another memory came, the feel of fingers tugging the three-carat princess cut diamond ring from my finger. Tears stung my eyes and every hair on my body stood on end. Of course, they'd taken it. They'd try to get money from Arthur now. Or my dad. They'd ransom me back, wouldn't they? I looked at the other women again. Were we all to be ransomed?

Moving the timeline up?

No fuck-ups, nothing linking back to me. Otherwise, make it look good.

That memory hurt. I closed my eyes and leaned back, warding off the sleep that wanted to claim me again, my head throbbing where a bump was, my neck tender. The truck drove fast and cars no longer passed us. I wasn't sure where we were or how long we'd been driving. I knew I'd been sedated, as I suspected the other girls had been — they too kept slipping in and out of consciousness.

Just as I was nodding off again, the sound of gunfire jolted all of us awake. Women screamed as something exploded in the distance, lighting up the black sky for a moment before a second, smaller explosion followed. The truck then swerved off the road, throwing us against one wall. Pain shot through my wrist, the chain linking the girl and me yanking at our arms. More gunfire rang out, along with the sound of men yelling. We all huddled onto the floor, covering our heads, many of the women weeping, screaming in terror.

I don't know why I remained silent, or how. Panic filled me and all I could do was count to keep my focus, to keep myself calm. I counted screams. I counted gunshots and prayed I wouldn't be killed in a spray of gunfire. I prayed like I had never prayed in my life.

A bullet ricocheted off the steel frame of the truck and that time I did scream. We held each other tightly and huddled as low as we could, making ourselves as small as possible until finally — an eternity later — it stopped.

It was nearly silent after that, the only sound the whimpering of the women. I peered out from between the steel slats of the enclosure wall, the tiny slit too small to get a good view outside. It was then I heard them. Two men talking, a door opening, something — or someone — falling with a loud thud.

"Fucking bastards," a rough male voice said.

Another replied but I couldn't make out the words. The voices were those of strangers. Were they our rescuers?

One more gunshot jolted us, the sound of metal on metal echoing through the truck as someone unlocked the door. The women huddled back. My eyes were glued to the door, my heart beating fast, dread of the unknown turning my blood cold. The door creaked as it opened from the top, rotating on the hinge at the bottom until it formed a sloping ramp down to the ground creating a sort of ramp used to load and unload animals. I could make out the form of a man — a large man — a weapon slung over his shoulder. It was too dark to see his face, but he shone a flashlight into the truck, the light stabbing through the blackness, blinding us. A few of the women screamed and he banged on the truck wall with the butt of his weapon.

"Settle down. No one's going to hurt you." His voice was deep and low, the sort of voice you felt rather than heard.

The women quieted to soft whimpering which he seemed to accept. He passed the light over us again and while the women cowered away, I remained still, looking straight at him, determined to make him look at me, to make him know I would fight. I knew somehow that this wasn't a rescue. I felt it. And the man standing at the door did nothing to change my mind. He shone that flashlight in my face and held it there until I heard a clicking of his tongue.

Suddenly, the headlights of an approaching vehicle blinded me, forcing me to look away.

When it came to a stop, the headlights flooded the interior of our truck, also illuminating the man who stood just outside it, the one who had opened the door. He was dressed in full black, his hair a shade darker than the night, his face impassive. He stared back at me, never once shifting his gaze, not to any of the others, not to the pickup truck now parked a few feet away. No, his gaze remained locked on mine, black eyes that made me tremble, that made the hairs on the back of my neck stand on end.

Footsteps approached, another man, bigger, his expression harder even as his golden eyes sparkled in the moonlight. He stood beside his partner, studying us, taking each girl in by turn before his eyes came to rest upon me. He looked at the first man, the pair exchanging whispered words before both of them turned to me again. A cold sweat broke out over my whole body. I could hear the faint sound of music from the pickup truck the second man had driven up in, the melody momentarily distracting me from the surreal situation. I recognized the song, the words of the chorus eerily appropriate to our predicament. We were the prey — and we'd been hunted by these men. Their gazes were impenetrable and predatory, the coldness in their eyes chilling.

I knew then that these men were not our rescuers. They, especially the one with eyes blacker than the night, radiated a single-minded purpose that instilled within me fear and fascination in equal measure. The similarity in their features was undeniable as I studied them standing beside one another. They were brothers. I had no doubt of that. And both of them stood studying me, focused intently only on me.

3

"Ladies," the man with the black eyes said, shifting his gun on his shoulder.

One of the women jumped. He glanced at her and she covered her face.

"Your captors are dead and you belong to us now. You're all going to stand up and quietly walk out of this truck and into that one there." He pointed, as if there were more than one truck to choose from. "You will remain silent. Is that clear?" He didn't wait for a reply. "You will not come to harm as long as you obey this simple instruction."

"Who are you?" I asked, the words out before I could think.

All eyes turned to me. My heart raced, realizing I'd just drawn the men's attention by disobeying this, their very first command. The one with the golden eyes simply stared, his gaze burning into me, but his brother — I decided to call him Obsidian then — exhaled loudly, and one corner of his lip turned upward.

"There's always one that just has to test, isn't there?" Obsidian asked in a whisper meant to be overheard. "It's so much more interesting when they do though, isn't it?" His gaze remained upon me even though he wasn't addressing me.

"Always," Golden Eyes said, only hardness etching his face.

"You will all learn that obedience is rewarded and disobedience punished. We'll make our first example once we reach camp." It was Obsidian who spoke, addressing the group with the threat meant for me.

I tried to swallow, but my mouth was a desert. A cold sweat covered me and after a long moment, I couldn't do it anymore, I couldn't hold their gazes and looked down to the floor of the truck. The woman I was chained to clutched my hand, her fingernails digging into my skin, our combined fear a palpable thing. I wondered if they could smell it on us even over the stench of animals that permeated the truck.

"If that's all the questions we have, then we'll get going, girls. Out." Golden eyes said.

On shaky legs, a dozen women slowly rose. A few still had shoes on; I wasn't one of them. Most wore clothes that were, perhaps not one or two nights ago, beautiful. Now they were tattered and filthy and had taken on the stench of the animals that must have been transported on this very truck before us.

They walked and I followed them, my companion and me the last off the truck. The two men nodded at each woman as they filed out and Golden Eyes loaded them into the back of the large pickup truck he had driven up in. Obsidian looked to be waiting just for me, and even as I tried to move as far from him as I could, when it was our turn to climb down off the truck, it wasn't possible. His gaze was like a physical thing, but he didn't touch me, and I held tight to the hand that held my own.

I made a mistake though when we were almost to the pickup truck. As my companion was climbing onto the back of it, I looked at the truck we'd just vacated. The cab was smashed, the bloody mess of the man who must have been driving our truck on the ground.

Panic crept into my mind, my soul, and I gasped for breath, my knees buckling beneath me. Golden Eyes' arm circled my waist, catching me before I fell, holding me upright.

"Easy."

My nose came to the middle of his very large, very wide chest. It hurt my neck to turn my face up to his, and even though I refused to cry, his image was blurred from the tears brimming inside my eyes.

He scanned my face, noting the bump on my forehead, and for a moment, I imagined I saw kindness in his gaze.

But I was mistaken.

"Up," he said, shifting his grip to my arm, lifting me to climb into the back of the truck. I sat next to the girl who shared my chain. She wept quietly, squeezing my hand as she did.

I determined not to look away then, not even when Obsidian returned with that smirk on his face, his eyes quickly fixing on me.

"Hope you're not going to be trouble," he said.

My friend's hand tightened around mine. I didn't reply.

"Or maybe I hope you are."

I swallowed, feeling the color drain from my face as I shivered.

He turned to the other man. "We're done here."

Golden Eyes nodded, made sure no fingers were in the way, and slammed the door shut. I exhaled then and leaned my head against my companion's shoulder.

We began to move, and I tried to look out the window. The glass was blacked out, and I could only make out the faint outline of the wrecked truck we'd been taken from.

These men were killers and although they had rescued us from what I was sure would have been a terrible fate, I had a feeling what they had in store for us would be a different sort of terrible.

But if I wanted to keep calm, I needed to distract myself.

"What's your name?" I asked the girl to whom I was bound.

"Lara."

"Lara, I'm Evangeline. Eva for short."

"Pretty name."

"Yours too."

She looked into my eyes, her big brown ones red, tears still flowing. "What's going to happen to us?"

I tried to keep the tremor from my voice, the tears from my eyes, but it took all I had to do it. "I don't know."

§

Gabriel drove, wrapped up in his own thoughts, neither he nor Syn speaking for the first twenty minutes.

"She rattled you," Syn finally said.

Gabriel kept his eyes on the road, his hands tightly gripping the steering wheel. "She seems different than the others. And familiar."

"I thought so too."

"I don't like dealing in humans," Gabriel said, glancing out the side window into wide, dark desert. There was nothing there, no one for miles. Arizona was the safest place to hijack cargo meant for the black market.

"Me either, but we don't have a choice, Gabe, and we

both know it. Besides, their fate won't be any worse than where they were going. Better, maybe."

Gabriel snorted. "No, just different. I still don't like it."

"You're heart isn't thawing, is it brother?"

Gabriel glanced at his younger brother, noting the usual dark glint in his eye. He wondered again if Syn enjoyed his work more than he should. For Gabriel, vengeance kept him alive.

"Collateral damage is a consequence of any war, Gabriel. These women drew the short straw, but even so, we're still their better option. Besides, it's our revenge. Every time we take over one of these shipments, whether it be drugs or human cargo, we take back a little of what they stole from us."

"We can't ever get her back, Syn, no matter how many of these shipments we hijack." Gabriel hardened his heart against the memory. He'd learned to do that over the years. If anything, he needed to remember what had happened to her, how she'd been found. That would give him power and strength. It would give him the drive to go on until every bastard who dealt in drugs and humans lay dead in a body bag.

SYN REACHED INTO HIS POCKET TO TAKE OUT HIS CELL PHONE. He dialed Remy, their associate who organized the auctions of the women, but his thoughts were on what was going on with his brother. He knew Gabriel didn't need Syn reminding him of what they'd lost six years ago when their sister, Laney, had turned up almost dead from an overdose. Syn hated the idea of selling the women as much as Gabriel did, but they had no choice and they both needed to keep their eyes on their goal, which was to eliminate men like Arthur Gallaston, the one from whom they had stolen tonight. They needed to bring him down, and people would get hurt in the process. It was an unpleasant fact, but they had to come to terms with it. Clearly, his brother hadn't yet.

Syn glanced over at Gabriel. Gabriel's flat gaze was fixed on the road ahead, the line of his mouth tight as he drove the truck to camp. He knew just what Gabriel felt. He felt it too every time they ambushed a shipment of women.

Remy finally picked up the phone.

"Syn," came Remy's voice.

"We've picked up the shipment, so the auction is a go. We've got thirteen girls. Make the calls, will you?"

"You got it, boss."

4

The sound of the cargo door opening woke most of us up. The sun was just rising, making me wonder how far we'd come from the city. Did my father know I was missing yet? What would he do when he found out?

I didn't have time to dwell on those questions though as we were slowly unloaded. The memory of what Obsidian had said only hours before still lay heavy on my mind:

Disobedience would be punished. An example would be made.

I shivered when I passed by Obsidian to stand in the still cool morning air, looking around as the rest of the women slowly climbed out, huddling together, awaiting further instruction. We weren't in the desert anymore, but in a large clearing in a forest. There were three large tents, several smaller ones and one mid-size RV. The larger tents were arranged at the center, the smaller ones bordering them to form a circle. Everything about the camp said primitive and temporary.

Several men stood around the camp, all with weapons

over their shoulders, all dressed in camouflage and looking to me like soldiers. The girls whimpered, each of them holding hands with the one they were bound to. It was the first time I got a good look at them in daylight and my impression of the night before had been correct — all of the women were attractive and young. The oldest was perhaps twenty-three, twenty-four. At not quite twenty-one yet, I was probably one of the youngest.

I looked at the two men who had rescued us from the cattle truck, who had then re-captured us. They were the ones in charge of the thirty or so soldiers who stood armed all around. They spoke in hushed tones with one of the soldiers who, after a few moments, nodded and walked off. Golden Eyes and Obsidian then turned their attention to us.

"Ladies," Obsidian said. "Follow me."

We did, following in a group to the clearing at the center of the circle of tents.

"Line up. Give me a nice straight row," he said.

The women began to move, me along with them, while two soldiers brought over a heavy-looking tree stump, placing it near Obsidian. Golden Eyes followed, carrying an ax at his side. All of us stared, open-mouthed. My mind raced, conjuring up the worst possible scenario, making me wonder if this was to be my punishment. If by "making an example" they meant to kill me in some brutal, barbaric fashion.

Lara squeezed my hand as if she could hear my thoughts while a quiet, panicked murmuring broke out among the women.

Golden Eyes stopped and turned to us. Placing thumb and forefinger into his mouth, he called us to attention with a loud whistle.

"Thank you, brother," Obsidian said.

I'd been right, they were brothers.

"Like hens, they can't stop clucking," he added.

I glared at him, at the callousness of his joke when he could clearly see our terror.

"Get on with it, Syn," Golden Eyes said.

Syn. Was that his name? What kind of a name was Syn?

"My brother's never been the most patient of men," Syn said, his tone flippant.

"You two." He pointed to the two women farthest from me to my left. "Come here."

It took him asking twice before the terrified women moved toward him.

"Kneel."

The girls knelt without a word.

He pointed to the tree stump. "Put your bound arms here, my brother will cut the chain."

My eyes grew wide as I realized how he meant to use the ax and we all watched while the two women raised trembling arms and set them down upon the stump.

"Take them as wide as you can but don't move," Golden Eyes said, checking the chain.

"I second that last part. Don't move," Syn said, grinning.

The terrified women did as they were told, and Syn gestured to two soldiers who stood nearby, giving them the command to hold onto the kneeling women's arms so they couldn't move. Golden Eyes raised the ax high and brought it down with a loud *thunk* onto the stump breaking the chain in one swift strike. The women screamed, and not just the ones who knelt with their arms on the stump. An inch or two in the wrong direction, and one of them would have lost a hand.

"Next," Syn said, gesturing for the women to return to the line, both rubbing their now free wrists.

They repeated this with each of the women and every time the ax came down, the ground rattled beneath our feet. When it was our turn, Lara and I knelt before the men and set our arms on the block of wood. I looked up at the brothers, at Golden Eyes holding the ax, taking Lara's arm a little farther from mine so the chain was taut.

Syn leaned down, brushing a strand of hair from my face, his cruel grin belying the gentleness of the gesture. "I haven't forgotten what I promised, in case you were wondering."

He straightened and nodded to the men who gripped our arms tightly. His brother measured out where the ax would fall. I glanced over at Lara who squeezed her eyes shut, and looked up in time to see Golden Eyes draw the ax over his head. His gaze was fixed on where he intended to strike, and when he brought the ax down, I couldn't help a small scream at the impact as the ax broke the chain that bound us.

"You, back in the line," Syn said to Lara as we rose to our feet. He took hold of my arm when I tried to follow her.

I looked at him, but when Lara reached out to squeeze my hand, I turned to her. Her eyes were wide, and I knew if she didn't go back into the line, she too would be punished.

"Go," I mouthed.

She squeezed harder before turning to take her place among the others. The one called Syn held on to me and I watched as one of the soldiers approached, carrying a handful of long, thin branches. I looked at the bundle, confused, then glanced at Syn. He met my gaze for a moment before turning his attention back to the women.

"My name is Syn," he began, then pointed to Golden

Eyes who held the ax. "This is my brother, Gabriel, but while we're all here together, you will simply call us 'Sir' when you are addressed — and only when you are addressed. You will be fed and clothed as long as you obey and do as you're told." He paused and glanced at me briefly. "Now, as I said earlier, obedience is rewarded, disobedience punished — and punished harshly."

When he returned his attention to me, I was surprised to see he wasn't smiling or gloating. He looked incredibly serious, almost as though he wasn't enjoying himself. But I wouldn't believe that.

His gaze ran the length of me. "What's your name?"

I looked from him to his brother and back, unable to answer until he shook me once.

"Name."

"Evangeline... Eva."

"Eva will be punished for her earlier disobedience. I suggest you all take her lesson to heart. I don't assume any of you have seen someone birched before?"

Birched?

My eyes grew wide at that, understanding what Syn meant to do, how he meant to punish me. The twigs the man had collected would be used as switches, bundled together and made into a birch rod. I'd then be whipped with them.

Panicked, I tried to pull my arm free of his grip, but he only squeezed harder, making me yelp.

"Take off your dress, Eva."

My heart pounded in my chest, a rushing sound in my ears.

"No!" I tried again to free myself, but he held tight. "Please don't. I didn't know."

"I realize that, but you'll know after this. Dress, Eva. Take it off. If I have to do it for you, it will be another show of disobedience, just to be clear."

I couldn't help but glance once more at the branches the man still held, my mind already working to count the number of sticks.

"Last chance, Eva."

My fingers trembled as I reached back to unzip my dress, but the zipper caught half way down. I looked at the women all standing in a row, watching, some already crying. The men at the periphery also watched, wide-eyed, their gazes lecherous, wholly different from those of the women. But I couldn't think of them, not now. I turned to Syn.

"It's stuck." Why did my voice sound so pathetically small?

He turned me around without a word and tugged on the zipper until it slid open. Then, without waiting for me to do it, he pushed the straps off my shoulders. All I could do was stand and watch as the once fine silk pooled at my feet in the dirt. I immediately covered my breasts with my arms as I wasn't wearing a bra, and my tiny thong left most of the rest of me exposed.

"Pretty," he said from behind me, a finger tracing the lace of the thong. He leaned in close, his face nearly touching mine. "But go ahead and take it off anyway."

The whispered words made me shudder.

The way he had positioned me kept me facing the others I'd been brought here with. Even as I knew they were not enjoying my shame, my cheeks still burned with embarrassment. But more than that was the knowledge of what was to come — the birching itself. I feared the punishment, the physical pain, but knew there was no way out of it. It was happening. It felt like this great bump in the road I had to climb over, that there was no way of circumventing, and it filled me with dread.

Trying not to think, I pushed the thong from my hips and stepped out of it to stand fully naked in front of everyone.

Syn walked around me, taking his time. Gabriel stood stoic in the background. Out of the two, Gabriel was bigger, stronger, but Syn with his leaner build and black eyes, seemed the crueler.

Once he'd enjoyed my naked form from every angle, Syn stood in front of me once more, his face inches from mine. I kept my gaze on his, wanting to show courage but fearing my trembling would give me away.

"Since this is your first time, I'll let you choose who takes the birch to that pretty little ass of yours — me or my brother."

He was letting me choose? I looked at the birch the soldier still held, then from Gabriel to Syn.

"Your brother." It took me two tries to say the words without my voice breaking, and I glanced once more in Gabriel's direction, hoping I'd chosen well.

Syn narrowed his eyes, but one corner of his mouth lifted into a smirk. "Too bad. But I imagine I'll get my turn soon. Kneel up on the tree stump, facing the others."

I went to the stump, unsure how he would position me, how much it would hurt, how humiliating this punishment would be, and I knelt on top of it, my gaze on the ground a few feet from me as I still tried in vain to cover myself.

Syn came to stand to my side and leaned down so his mouth was at my ear. "Now, I can hold you down for this, but I'd like for you to submit to your punishment as an example to the rest over there." He spoke so that only I could hear his words. "If I have to make you take it, then you'll watch as each girl takes a turn right here where you kneel now and they'll all know whose fault it was. Understand?"

"I've never... no one has... please don't do this. I'm sorry." My pleading embarrassed me, but for the moment, fear overrode pride.

He smiled. "Shh. I had the boys peel the branches for you."

Peel the branches? What did that mean?

Syn placed a hand at my neck and I watched Gabriel step forward and take the birch from the soldier before coming to stand at my side. I looked up at Gabriel.

"I think you chose wrong," he said before turning his attention to the branches, rearranging them, pulling one from the bunch and discarding it after finding a bump.

Again, just as the night before, I'd hoped he would show mercy. And again, I was disappointed.

Gabriel nodded to his brother who pushed me forward.

"Bend down, hands on the ground, ass pushed out for my brother to whip," Syn said.

"Please don't!" I fought him, trying to free myself, but he only squeezed my neck harder. "I didn't know. I'm sorry! Please don't hurt me!"

"Take it easy, brother," Gabriel said, intervening. "She's scared."

It took a moment, but Syn released me and took a step back. "Fine."

Gabriel turned to me. "Evangeline," he said, using my full name, imploring me with his eyes to look at him while mine brimmed with tears. "You're going to be punished. How you choose for that to happen is up to you. I realize you're afraid. You don't know us, you've been taken from your home, your family perhaps, but this is your new life.

The sooner you understand that, the better off you'll be. You will obey Syn. You will obey me, and you will obey whichever master who buys you."

"Buys me?" Tears streamed free from my eyes now.

Gabriel brought a hand to the back of my head and caressed my hair. It was the most tender, most gentle touch I'd ever felt, and in that moment, I trusted him. My brain screamed at the stupidity of that trust, but my gut said yes.

"Shh now. Let's take it one step at a time. I can't let you off the hook — it wouldn't set a good example — but if you're a good and obedient girl, I'll see about getting you some ointment after your whipping. Understand?"

He was still caressing me and I sniffled loudly, wiping tears away with the backs of both hands.

"Now, I need you to bend down and put your hands on the ground. You'll need to do that to brace yourself so you don't fall forward when I strike. Can you do that for me? For the others so they don't find themselves in this same predicament?"

I tasted my own blood as my teeth worked my lip, but I nodded.

"Good girl," he said. "I'll even help you down."

The stump was low enough that I wasn't quite upside down, but high enough so that I wouldn't have been able to do it on my own. With Gabriel's help, my hands were flat on the ground and my bottom raised up high, all of me exposed to whoever stood behind me.

"I'll give you an even dozen, Evangeline. Be good now."

Not a moment passed between his words and the first stroke. I thought I'd die when it landed, the ten or so twigs bundled together biting into me as one, covering the whole surface of my bottom, feeling like ten separate lashes. I didn't make a sound louder than a gasp at the first one, but the second had me crying out and those cries only grew worse as Gabriel punished me. No one spoke. In fact, the only sounds were those of the birch striking, of Gabriel's breathing as he laid on stroke after stroke, of the weeping of the girls forced to watch me being made an example of.

"Half way," he said.

Half way. I was going to die. It was impossible to hold my position. I felt a hand at my low back, pressing on it, steadying me while at the same time, forcing my bottom higher. But that hand also rubbed a slow circle, and somehow reassured, and although I took the next six strokes without any grace, I managed to remain in position. No one else would have to endure this because of me. I would take it. I would take the punishment so no one else would have to.

When it was over, two sets of hands lifted me back up to my knees, and with an arm around my waist, Gabriel hauled me to my feet. I wept as he held me with one arm, supporting me fully, allowing me to hide my face in his chest.

I didn't realize he was turning me to show the others the result of my punishment until I heard their gasps, but I already knew it was bad. The throbbing burn and sting were like nothing I'd ever felt before. I'd never even been hand spanked as a child, much less birched.

"It hurts," I said, hiding my face in his chest, tentatively reaching back to touch my sore, tender bottom.

"I imagine it does," Gabriel said, taking my hands and pulling them away. "But there are worse things than a birching, Evangeline."

I looked up to find him studying me, and saw only concern in his eyes now. I wondered what he meant by what he said, that there were worse things than a birching. Was it a threat? Somehow, I didn't think so. There was a tender, raw pain in his eyes that called to me. I wanted to know more. I wanted to know him, this man, this giant of a man who could beat me in one breath and hold me so tenderly in the next.

5

Gabriel reluctantly handed her to one of the girls, the one she'd been bound to originally, who also picked up her discarded clothes and covered her as best as she could while walking her back to the line. Evangeline went, but turned to glance once more at him. He held her gaze until she looked away.

The switches he'd used now lay innocuously on the ground by the stump. He kicked them away, the image of her kneeling so obediently before him, bent deeply, offered for his punishment, burned a permanent image into his mind. He'd not whipped a woman in a very long time. Syn took more pleasure from that, and Gabriel didn't mind leaving it to him. But today, when she'd chosen him rather than his brother to punish her, something had stirred inside him. Something alongside the thickening of his cock at the thought of whipping her, at the sight of her naked body, her bared bottom spread for him, the glimpse of her pretty pink pussy from between her cheeks, her sweet submission. Granted, she'd chosen him thinking he might be the lesser of two evils, but he hoped she'd learned today that there was no lesser, not between himself and his brother.

Gabriel didn't like what he had to do with the girls, but their fate had been sealed when Gallaston had chosen them for his cargo. At least when Gabriel sold them, he would know they were safe, or he hoped so anyway. Either way, they had no choice. In Gabriel's world, choice was a privilege, not a right.

Gabriel looked up to find Syn watching him, the expression in his eyes more inquisitive than harsh. Syn had changed over the years. He had hardened. His heart had grown a little colder, a little darker. But Gabriel couldn't blame him, could he?

"She's under your skin, brother," Syn said, adjusting the crotch of his pants. "It's been a long time since a woman's gotten under your skin."

"And yours," Gabriel said, bending to pick up the branches to busy himself, not wanting to meet his brother's eyes.

"Nah. Just a nice piece of ass."

Gabriel stopped and turned to Syn. "They're all a nice piece of ass. Gallaston has good taste. There's something about her that's got your attention though. Don't deny it."

Emotion flashed through Syn's eyes but he was quick to shield it. "Well, she'll likely be gone fast anyway. No way the men Remy's lining up for the auction will pass her up."

Gabriel's mouth tightened. Although Remy was trustworthy, Gabriel didn't want to know the details of how he came to know the men who would be bidding on the girls.

Syn stood watching him. That was the trouble with Syn, he could always read what Gabriel was thinking and vice versa. They were close, had been since they were kids. There was only a year difference between them and they were used to being together, trusting only each other.

"When are they coming?" Gabriel asked. The plan was to sell the girls, and no matter how unsavory the thought was, they had to do it. And he knew that as much as Syn tried to act casual about it, he didn't like it any more than Gabriel did.

"Over the next few days."

"Remy's screened them?"

"Always, brother. You ready to tell them what's going on?"

Gabriel nodded, his face tight. "May as well get it over with."

"We've never kept one," Syn said while they walked, his gaze straight ahead.

Gabriel's thoughts were in exactly the same place, but there wasn't room for that line of thinking. "And we're not going to start."

He walked off toward the RV to find the ointment he'd promised Evangeline.

᠅

Syn stared after his brother. Gabriel could be a real pain in the ass sometimes. Syn often wondered if Gabriel realized he wasn't the only one who suffered after Laney's overdose. She was his sister too, even if she and Gabe had been closer.

Grinning, he walked to the tent where the girls had been led to bathe. He rather enjoyed this part. Thirteen beautiful women stripped naked and made to wash while he watched. His cock stiffened at the thought.

They didn't notice him, at least not at first. They all stood huddled around Eva, two helping her pull her dress on, others comforting her, one standing away from the group, her gaze sending daggers into the punished girl's back. He shook his head. Women. She'd just been stripped and beaten publicly and there was already jealousy? He'd never understand the opposite sex.

He turned to find the three large barrels being filled with water. Getting water to the site was a pain in the ass, but he couldn't exactly auction off the girls when they stank of a barn, and inevitably, every shipment did.

Syn pulled up the chair behind the table he'd use as a desk and whistled them to attention. "Line up facing me."

All talking ceased and the girls shuffled to do as he said while he opened a leather bound notebook on the desk, turning to an empty page. He then looked up at the row of beautiful women before him. He liked this part. He liked it much more than he should, but he had no problem with that darker part of himself. He'd come to terms with it the day they had pronounced Laney brain-dead. The same day he and Gabriel both had sworn vengeance.

"Name," he said, pointing to the first girl with his pen. "First, middle and last."

"Maria Anna Calvares," came the trembling voice of the girl.

"Maria." He looked her over from head to toe. "Lose the dress, Maria."

She started to cry right away, and Syn shook his head. But what he saw next truly surprised him. Eva stepped forward from the line and folded her arms across her chest.

"If you'd tell us what was going to happen to us, maybe we'd be more cooperative. In case you're too stupid to realize it, she's scared, asshole!"

There was a collective intake of breath from the women.

One girl reached to pull her back into the line, but Eva shrugged off her hand, staring at Syn even as her legs trembled and her pretty, gray-green eyes widened in anticipation of what he'd do next.

Syn stood, and when he rounded the desk, she took a step back.

"Haven't heard a woman call my brother an asshole in… well, I believe this may be the first time, actually." Gabriel stood at the entrance of the tent with a smile on his face. "You have to admit," he said, walking inside, setting a small jar and a camera on the desk. "It is true, Syn." Gabriel patted his brother's back.

"May be true, but it's also rude."

"Yes, it is that."

"Eva, I'm going to forgive that little outburst only if you get your pretty little ass back in line. Unless of course you'd like me not to forgive it? Perhaps you'd like another dozen to top off the whipping which my brother obviously didn't do a good enough job with?" Syn asked, sending a sideways glance at Gabriel.

She narrowed her eyes, the green darkening. "I just… we just want to know what's going to happen to us. Please." She then hastily added, "I don't mean disrespect."

"That's better," he said, turning to his brother. "Almost sweet, wouldn't you say?"

"She does seem sweet," Gabriel said, his eyes on the girl. "Back in line with the others, Evangeline. And this goes for all of you. As Syn said earlier, you'll address us as Sir and only speak when spoken to. We'll do it like school. If you have a question, raise your hand. You clear on that, Evangeline? I don't want to give my brother an excuse to take the birch, or anything else for that matter, to that pretty little ass of yours. I know he's dying to."

Syn smiled just a little. This was what he respected so thoroughly about his brother. He could be intensely serious, and was most of the time, he had a soft heart, softer than he himself did, but when push came to shove, he always had your back. He could charm anyone, if he chose to. They both could. It was just that Syn didn't feel the need to most of the time.

Eva nodded and stepped back in line with the other women.

"Now," Gabriel said, folding his arms across his chest and looking at the girl with a tilt of his head. "How do you reply respectfully, do you think?"

Syn tried hard not to chuckle as he watched her hands clench into fists, her eyes narrow to slits.

"Yes... sir," she spat.

"That's a good girl. Take note, ladies." With that, Syn resumed his place behind the makeshift desk and Gabriel pulled up a chair to sit beside him.

❧

I was fuming. I was going to kill him. I was going to kill them both.

My nails bit into my palms and Lara whispered a quick "let it go" into my ear, earning herself a look from Syn.

I blew out a long breath. They held the power now. I would do what I had to do to survive this, and when I had the chance, I'd kill both of the smug, arrogant assholes. I shook my head at myself. What had I been thinking earlier taking comfort in Gabriel's embrace? And after he'd whipped me? After he'd humiliated me like that?

Trust your gut.

My gut was off, obviously.

Gabriel kept his eyes on mine and shook his head once. I glared at him, but when he raised his eyebrows, I forced myself to look at a point beyond his left shoulder.

"You want to know what's going to happen to you, but first let me tell you what *would* have happened to you had we allowed that cattle truck you were on to reach its destination and deliver its cargo. You would have been sold most likely to a whorehouse someplace where pretty, young American girls are highly sought after. You'd be a prisoner and at the mercy of whichever asshole ran the show over there for the rest of your lives, and I have a feeling they wouldn't be long lives. You'd be on your back or on your knees servicing some prick with the cash to afford a quick fuck or maybe just a suck. This is how you would live and how you would die. Am I clear? Are there any questions so far?"

He looked at me when he asked the last part but any joking had vanished from both his tone and his face. I believed what he said. I believed every word of it.

"I won't tell you that what's going to happen to you now will be a piece of cake," Syn continued.

I looked up to find both men watching me. I tried not to show my fear, tried not to show any emotion at all. I needed to harden myself. I couldn't be weak, not if I wanted to survive.

"But I can promise you safety and a settlement of cash."

"What?" someone asked quietly.

I glanced down the row of women, all the faces I saw confused.

"This here is my ledger," Syn said, holding up the notebook. "I will write down each of your names and ages here. Beginning later today, men will come—"

A loud chorus of cries and protests arose from the gathered women, but Syn continued.

"You will sign a contract agreeing be sold for a period of three years."

"No!" A few women called out.

"All of the men have been screened, and you will belong to them. During the three years, they will keep you safe, and, for the most part, very well cared for. These are wealthy, influential men. You will want for nothing."

"Nothing but our freedom!" one of the women, a pretty blonde, called out.

Gabriel moved fast, approaching the woman who'd spoken out. She tried to duck away but he caught her easily, turned her so her back was to us while he held her to him, and spanked her hard three times until she cried out.

"What's your name?" he asked, forcing her to look at him.

"Leslie," she managed through tears.

"Leslie, get your ass back in line and keep your mouth shut while my brother is talking. Clear?"

"Perhaps Eva, you can show Leslie what happens..." Syn offered, gesturing for me to turn around.

"Not necessary, brother," Gabriel said, his eyes on mine.

Leslie scrambled back to her spot.

"You're no fun," Syn said to Gabriel.

"Wrap it up, Syn."

Syn shook his head but I could see there was no animosity between the brothers.

"At the end of your term with your Master, you will be given your freedom along with a healthy amount of cash that, if you're smart, will allow you to live comfortably for the rest of your lives. So to wrap it up, as my brother so neatly said, you *will* be sold, and if you do what is expected of you, you will not be harmed. You will regain your freedom once the term of three years is up. Now, you have to admit that's a better deal than what you had going in."

Was he really trying to make light of this?

"Any questions?"

Lara raised her hand and waited until Syn nodded at her to proceed. "Can we say no, sir?"

He shook his head.

"I want to go home."

It was my turn to comfort her now and I hugged her to me as she wept.

Neither brother commented but after a few moments, Syn spoke again, addressing Maria, the first girl in line.

"Let's try this again. Maria. Step forward."

The girl took a tentative step and Gabriel snapped a photo of her face.

"Strip off your clothes. You won't be needing them anymore," Syn said.

The teary-eyed, petite Maria did as she was told. Once he'd written the information down in his book, she was sent to the barrels that stood waiting for us — our bath. We would be sharing the water until the stench of the last twenty-four hours was scrubbed off of us.

"Eva," Syn said when it was my turn. His gaze ran the length of me. "Strip. Age and last name."

"Twenty. Evangeline Roberts," I lied. I didn't even know why. Would it have mattered to them if they knew who I was? Would they try to extort money from my dad? Or would it possibly save me? Would I be more valuable to them then?

Syn studied me for a while and I wondered if he knew I

was lying. I tried to keep my gaze upon his but could only manage to look at his forehead instead. I didn't like lying and had never been very good at it. I just hoped he wouldn't catch me doing it. I had on doubt the punishment would be severe.

6

"She's lying." Syn said.

"I know," Gabriel replied.

The brothers walked to the RV, which they used as an office as it was connected to a power generator. The girls were settled in one of the large tents and given something to eat. They'd stay there until a little before the buyers came, when they'd be collected and told what would be expected of them during the auction.

Gabriel and Syn sat down behind their desks and Syn opened his laptop. They'd go through the names to match up the girls, make sure no one had lied. Fortunately, lying was rarely an issue as the girls were too afraid to do it, but it paid to check anyway. They'd then register them and confirm there wouldn't be any problems with the shipment of women.

They worked quickly and quietly, splitting the list of women. Gabriel was called out by one of the soldiers, and by the time he returned, Syn was finished with his half of the list and was already searching missing persons reports to verify what they both believed.

He wasn't expecting to find what he found though.

"You aren't going to believe this," Syn said.

"What?" Gabriel asked, rolling his chair backward to where Syn pointed to his computer screen. "You're fucking kidding me."

"They just filed the missing person's report. Press conference started a few minutes ago."

"I don't believe it."

There on the screen was a picture of Eva's pretty face all lit up with a wide smile. She was on the arm of her fiancé on the night of their engagement, according to the report. Then came another photo, this one of her with her family at the White House. Evangeline Roberts was actually Evangeline Webb, daughter of Senator Victor Webb of the Long Island Webb's, a wealthy political family with ties to Arthur Gallaston.

And the closest ties of all were those of the girl the brothers now held captive. Evangeline Webb was Arthur Gallaston's fiancée.

Syn and Gabriel watched in silence as the press conference began. Eva's father was visibly shaken, but her fiancé looked a little too composed, as if he were affecting shock. And now they knew exactly why. This shipment was one of Gallaston's. They had expected a dozen women, but there had been thirteen on board. Evangeline had to have been a last minute addition.

The reports claimed she'd gone for a run after the fundraiser the night before but had never returned to the hotel. Her fiancé had only discovered her disappearance in the morning when he'd woken to find she wasn't in bed beside him.

"Please," Gallaston spoke into the camera, his voice

cracking with contrived emotion. "If you have her, please don't hurt her. Bring her home. Please."

Her father was unable to speak, his sorrow very different from that of Arthur Gallaston. The older man looked almost broken.

A spokesman came forward and spoke of the reward being offered for any information leading to Eva's safe return.

This didn't make sense. It was a set-up. It had to be. Or had Gallaston arranged to have his own fiancée kidnapped? This was much more complex than what Gallaston planned to do with the other women. When selecting women for the black market, it was easier to choose those who wouldn't be missed, women from lower socio-economic classes, those without much family. Evangeline Webb would not disappear quietly. She would be missed. And her family held entirely too much power and too much money to allow her disappearance to be brushed under the carpet, no matter who was doing the brushing.

Neither Syn nor Gabriel spoke until the press conference was over. Gabriel stood, running a hand through his hair, and walked to the small window, gazing out onto the tent where the girls were housed. Syn switched off the computer and turned his chair to face his brother.

"What the hell do you think happened? I mean Gallaston is a son of a bitch, but to put his own fiancée on a truck to be sold into sexual slavery? Doesn't make sense, especially given who her father is."

Gabriel rubbed the back of his neck and leaned against the RV wall to face Syn. "Or maybe she was part of it all from the start."

"No." Syn shook his head. "I don't believe that."

Gabriel's eyes narrowed. "We can't rule it out."

Theirs To Take

"Then why is she here?"

"I don't know. Maybe she got cold feet. Maybe she pissed Gallaston off."

"Or maybe she found out what he was up to and he panicked," Syn suggested.

"Well, I imagine he's even more panicked now that the cargo's been hijacked," Gabriel said with a grin. "Evangeline Webb has some explaining to do. And she's going to learn that lying to us is not a good idea."

"Gabe..." Syn began. "I don't believe she's a part of this. My gut tells me that."

Someone knocked on the door, interrupting their conversation.

"Come in," Gabriel said.

The door opened and one of the soldiers stuck their head inside. "Boss, we've got the first of the buyers arriving this evening."

Of course they were. When talk of a human auction was circulated, they came fast, knowing the cream of the crop would be taken first.

"All right. Get the girls out and lined up. If any of them gives you any trouble, you know what to do." Gabriel gestured to the canes that stood in an umbrella stand by the door.

"Yes, sir," the guard said, choosing one of the long sticks. The glint in his eye let Syn know that not only wouldn't he mind having to put one of the girls in line, he hoped he'd have to.

"Make sure you don't touch Eva," Syn added to Gabriel's command. "Bring her with the rest of them but don't touch her, understand?" He felt Gabriel's eyes on him but ignored his brother.

"Yes, sir," the soldier said.

At Gabriel's nod of dismissal, the soldier left, closing the door behind him. Gabriel then turned to Syn.

"Either way," Gabriel said, continuing their conversation before the guard had come in. "Looks like we'll be keeping one after all."

Syn nodded, picked up a cane and walked out of the RV. They'd be selling one less girl today, but that girl could prove to be more valuable than the dozen put together. Whatever the reasons for keeping her would be, all he felt at the prospect of it was excitement.

≈

A FEW HOURS EARLIER, WE HAD BEEN TAKEN TO A TENT, WHICH contained a mat and a thin blanket for each of us.

Lara and I lay on our mats as most of the women did. Some spoke but most were either quiet or trying to sleep. Every few minutes, the sound of someone crying would disturb the rest of the group. Lara and I talked a little bit. She came from Minnesota, had come to Phoenix to visit a friend for a few days. Now she wondered if she'd ever see her parents or her kid brother ever again.

"You think they're looking for us?" she asked.

Sadness filled me. How would anyone ever find us?

"I'm sure they are, Lara."

"But they won't find us, will they? I mean—" she began to cry again. "I don't even know how long we drove. If we're even in Arizona — or the US — anymore."

"Tell me about your family," I asked, trying to get her mind off things.

"There's my mom and dad and my little brother. He's only ten. I promised to bring him back a Cardinals jersey. I'd already bought it." A fresh onslaught of tears rendered her unable to speak.

"It'll be okay, Lara. You'll see."

She shook her head, wiping her nose with her worn tissues. "They probably don't even know I'm missing yet."

"Why don't you just shut it?" A woman's voice said loudly.

I bristled. Clearly, the comment was directed at Lara. I turned to find the girl who'd spoken, a pretty blonde sitting several cots away on her own watching us. Or more, glaring at us. It was strange how even in a time like this, where we were all in the same horrible predicament, there was still room for cruelty.

"Why don't *you* shut it," I said, hugging Lara closer.

"You all need to stop your whining. Three fucking years and we'll be set for life. You heard him."

"And you believed him?" I shook my head. "How can you even think that's okay?"

"It's better than where I came from."

"Well, it's not better than where I came from."

"I guess not, princess. I saw the dress you had on the night we were brought here. I know Versace when I see it." She made a point of scanning me from head to toe. "Not so hot here though, are you?" she said, standing, her eyes filled with a hate I couldn't understand. This woman was a stranger to me.

All the girls quieted and I stood. "What the hell is your problem?" I took a step toward her but Lara grabbed my hand, holding me back.

The girl grinned and closed the space between us. "My problem is rich girls like you thinking you're better than me."

I stared at her, flabbergasted. "I... what? In case you don't realize it, we were all taken against our will. We're in the same boat. Equal."

"I don't know, watching you get your ass whipped sure put a smile on my face."

I pulled my hand out of Lara's when the blonde butted her shoulder against mine, shoving me backward.

"You fucking bitch! I took that so he wouldn't do it to any of you," I said, pushing her right back.

Her grin only widened. She was getting to me, and she knew it. I was letting her win. But then I realized something. As impossible as it was, I understood it.

"Wait, you're not jealous, are you?" I asked.

That wiped the smile right off her face and she would have lunged at me except that in that moment, Syn came walking into the tent. The instant he saw we were about to fight, he swung the cane he held, managing to hit both of us at once with the short, quick flick of his wrist. We both gasped, turning to him, our hands covering the spot he'd hit.

"You causing trouble again, Eva?" he asked.

"She called me a fucking bitch," the blonde called out. "She was going to fight me!"

"You started it!"

"She did. It's true," Lara chimed in, standing, the tension in the room thick.

"Settle down. Everyone sit but you two." He pointed his stick at the blonde. "Helena."

"Yes, sir," Helena answered demurely.

He turned back to the girls who remained standing. "I said sit."

I'd never seen a group of women drop so quickly at a command. Syn approached us, his eyes on mine.

"Is it true? Did you call her a fucking bitch, Eva?"

I searched his gaze for clues to his mood, but his expression was coolly impassive. "Yes."

"Yes, what?"

I pressed my lips together, exhaling, my hands curling into fists at my sides. "Yes, *sir*."

"Better. We'll make this easy." He handed the cane to Helena who took it. "Eva, Turn around, bend over, and lift your dress. Then put your hands on the mattress."

I looked from him, to the cane, to Helena, who was having a hard time keeping the smirk off her face. I wondered if he saw it.

"Sir..." one of the girls began.

I looked at her. It was Maria, the quiet one. Syn glared at her. "I'd suggest keeping your mouth shut unless you'd like to join Eva here, Maria."

Maria's nervous gaze flitted from him, to me, to Helena before she lowered it and stepped back. Syn turned his attention back to me.

"Eva?"

I turned my back to Helena and slowly bent over, lifting my dress to expose my bottom as I did. I then placed my hands on the mattress as he'd ordered. My heart raced, my bottom tensed in anticipation, the pain of my birching still too fresh.

"You hold on to her," he said to Lara. "If she moves her hands to cover herself, you'll be punished as well. Understood?"

Tears slid down Lara's face as she crouched down in front of me, covering my hands with hers. "I'm sorry," she murmured.

I kept my gaze down, staring at the ground, awaiting my sentence.

"Three strokes, Helena. Keep them off her thighs."

"Yes, sir. Thank you, sir."

I squeezed my eyes shut as I saw her move into position to the side of me before lining up the cane against my bottom. She rubbed it along my flesh, dragging this out, so obviously enjoying my humiliation.

I tensed everything when she drew her arm back and knew I'd never forget the sound of the cane when she brought it down hard across the center of my ass. I called out, an exhale turning into a gasp, then a bitten off scream as the pain exploded. The cane burned a stripe across my bottom, intensifying as the moments passed, the skin itself feeling tight and raw where she'd struck.

"Count, Eva — and thank Helena."

I hated him. "One. Thank you."

"She's learning. Don't go over the same spot," he directed her as she lined up the next stroke just below the first, seeming entirely too experienced with the cane.

She swung again, the pain even more terrible than the first now that I knew what it would be like. I forced myself to keep silent even as the tears squeezed from my eyes. "Two. Thank you."

"I'm impressed," Syn said. "Last one. Make it count. This is a good spot," he said, his fingers coming to the crease between my bottom and thighs.

The final stroke was the hardest of all and I heard Helena grunt with its delivery. Lara pressed down hard on my hands then and it took all I had not to move out of position. Lara's face was only a few inches from mine, her cheeks wet with tears, her sympathetic weeping having increased with each stroke that fell.

"Three," I exhaled, out of breath. "Thank you."

I remained as I was while Syn's fingers traced the welts softly. "Will you ever call Helena a fucking bitch again, Eva?"

"No, sir," I said, desperate now to be let up, to cover myself, to rub my poor, punished bottom.

"Good girl. Straighten up now. And don't rub."

I stood, my face feeling hot when I met first his gaze, then Helena's. Her eyes glowed bright with victory.

"Helena, hand the cane to Eva."

"What?" the blonde asked, pulling back.

"Well, I assume she didn't just call you a fucking bitch out of the blue. There is no black or white in life. Only gray. And I find the cane to be a perfect way to deal with all of that gray."

"But..."

"Hand it to her. Now. Then turn around, bend over and raise your skirt. You," he pointed at one of the women. "You'll hold her down while she takes her strokes."

I stood with my mouth open, trying to process, trying to keep my hands at my sides rather than rubbing the pain from my bottom. He wanted me to cane her?

"Syn..." Helena began in her most seductive voice.

He shook his head. "Sir. It's 'sir.' Now hand over the cane, bend over and take your punishment with the grace Eva showed us."

I couldn't believe my eyes as she reluctantly offered me the cane. When I simply stood staring at it, Syn took hold of my wrist, and pressed it into my hand.

"I can't," I said, holding the cane out to him. "I don't want to. Sir."

I felt Helena's gaze burning into me but I kept my eyes on Syn who looked confused.

"You're saying you don't want to give back what she gave you?"

The entrance flaps of the tent flipped back, and Gabriel stepped inside, his keen gaze assessing the situation.

I raised my chin, determined I would not do this, and met Syn's gaze. "No, sir. I... would not."

He studied me for what felt like an eternity and I wondered what I'd do if he made me cane her or made me take more strokes until I was willing to punish Helena back. Could I do that? Would I?

"I'm sorry, but I won't."

This was who I was. This was who I would remain, even in captivity.

Syn nodded and took the cane back. He turned to one of the soldiers who stood by. "Take them outside."

The girls all filed out slowly and I followed, feeling Gabriel's gaze on me as I made my way out of the tent. Helena didn't join us and it wasn't long after that that I heard the sounds of female cries coming from inside the tent. I didn't feel happy about it. I didn't gloat. I felt like crying with her, even if she had been wrong, even if she had been horrible to both Lara and me. She was a victim, like the rest of us.

Sadness overcame me when I saw a teary-eyed and naked Helena approach with her hands at the back of her head, joining us in the line. Even though she glared daggers at me, I only wanted to cry at the hopelessness of our situation.

7

"Single file, eyes on me," Gabriel began. "Let's go."

We all turned from Helena to him while she took her place at the end of the line, her hands still clasped at the back of her head. Syn followed her out, holding the cane casually at his side, no smile on his face, nothing that would hint at him having enjoyed punishing Helena. He did make a point of looking directly at me though as if to say something, to send some message. All I knew was that in that moment, I wasn't afraid of him — but I also didn't hate him. I somehow found him to be just, as insane as the notion seemed given the circumstances.

"Evangeline, are you having difficulty hearing me?" Gabriel asked.

One corner of Syn's lip turned up and he shook his head, as if expecting me to disobey.

I snapped my gaze to Gabriel. "No."

"No, what?"

My whole body shuddered at his question. I fisted my hands and my belly tensed. He waited, but he didn't have to wait long as the fresh, still throbbing stripes on my bottom reminded me what would happen if I did not obey these men. "No, sir."

He nodded. "Good girl." He resumed addressing the group. "The first set of buyers will be here by the end of the day."

Murmurs broke out among the women. Gabriel silenced them with a stern look.

"You *will* be ready for them. First order of business — you saw what happened in the tent a few moments ago, yes?"

All heads nodded.

"If you disobey during the auction, no questions will be asked, no second chances given. You will be led to a corner and caned on the spot. It will be very painful and very public. Is that clear?"

Several of the women looked at me, then at Helena who still held her hands at the back of her head, her tears beginning anew.

"I think they have cotton in their ears, Syn. Maybe they need motivating?"

"Pleasure, brother," Syn said, tapping the cane against his leg while walking toward us.

"Yes, sir!" we all called out in unison, making both brothers smile.

"Good. First thing, strip off your dresses. You'll be naked from now until the end of the auction. Potential buyers need to see the goods before making their choices."

He waited while we reluctantly pulled the simple white tunic like dresses up over our heads, a guard walking down the line collecting them from each of us. Both Syn and Gabriel scanned the row of now naked women.

"Good. During inspections, you'll be expected to hold your hands the way Helena is, clasped at the back of your head. Assume the position now, please. Make space in the line as you need to."

There was more hesitation from the women at this command than there had been about stripping. This felt so... exposed. So vulnerable. And as I looked at the women around me beginning to assume the required position, and even while my own arms moved upward, the fingers of my right hand lacing through those of the left, there was an undeniable fluttering of my belly, something that happened rarely, something that accompanied the heat that flared between my legs.

This was wrong. *I* was wrong. How could I become aroused by this degradation?

"Good." He turned to his brother. "Is Clara ready?"

Clara? Who was Clara and what was she ready for?

"Always. She'll be busy," Syn said, looking down the row.

"We'll do this in two sets, six in one group, seven in the other," Gabriel said, pointing to some of the women in the line, including me. "You six, head into that tent there." He indicated one of the larger tents I hadn't been inside yet. "Clara will get you shaved bare."

My mouth fell open. *Shaved bare?* I'd always had a modest bikini wax but never anything like that.

As I was the last in the line, I followed the others and Syn walked behind me, staying close to us.

"Hands at the backs of your heads, ladies, until you're excused from the position. Best to get used to it."

I hadn't realized my hands were slipping but we all straightened up quickly. Inside the tent, a woman who looked to be in her mid-fifties sat waiting for us. She spoke in Spanish to Syn who spoke fluently back. She then called the first girl and pointed to the low bench before her. The girl sat, and the woman continued speaking to her in Spanish, though it was obvious the girl couldn't understand a word of what was being said. Unfortunately, I did understand. Finally, Syn began to translate to the frightened girl.

"Spread your legs wide. She's going to shave your pussy. All of it. You can lower your arms and use them to support you as you lean backward to make it easier for Clara. It might also be more comfortable for you."

I couldn't help a glance at him. That was real kindness coming from him.

The girl spread her legs wide and leaned backward as instructed. The woman went to work. She didn't speak, instead, she lathered on foam and shaved the girl as if she'd done this a hundred times before, and perhaps she had. The front was done in no time and the woman gave the next instruction, which Syn translated.

"On your hands and knees, legs wide again, your bottom to Clara so she can get the back shaved."

The girl's face turned bright red and she turned an imploring gaze up to Syn.

"Move," he said.

She obeyed, getting onto all fours, her bottom fully and humiliatingly exposed to the woman.

"Arch your back," Syn said, coming to stand over Clara's shoulder. Of course he would. Why not get a good look? The girl obeyed but clearly didn't arch enough because Clara said something over her shoulder. Syn moved around to press on the girl's lower back, forcing her bottom high. "Like this. Hold the position. Clara's razors are very sharp. You don't want her to cut you."

The mortified girl's face flushed a deep red as Clara went to work, pulling one cheek out wider, smearing foam over the girl's most intimate parts and shaving. All this time, I watched, unable to look away.

It was over within a few moments and Syn tapped the girl's hip with the cane. "You can go back and rejoin the others." He then turned to us. "Next."

Another girl stepped up, each order obeyed. I watched each of them, utterly and shamefully fascinated. I'd never been attracted to women. I found them beautiful, but I'd never been drawn to one sexually — and I wasn't now — but my arousal was undeniable, my sex feeling hot.

And I realized that when it was my turn to get into position, I wouldn't be able to hide that arousal from Syn's gaze.

"Ah, Eva," Syn said a few moments later. "Your turn. Have a seat."

I did, and I spread my legs wide, knowing there was no way out of it and wanting it over as quickly as possible. The foam was cool and when she smeared it over me, it felt strange, the manner in which she worked too cool for so intimate an act. Although I'd been aroused watching the other women being shaved, her touch wasn't sexual to me. It was the idea of the others watching me that titillated.

She was quick, moving the razor expertly over my delicate folds, and when she was finished, she told me to turn over.

"Can you at least go away for this part? Please. Sir." The last word I added with reluctance, not truly expecting him to do it.

"I'd really love to stay and watch, actually. Hands and knees, Eva. We need you shaved bare front to back."

Why his words made my nipples harden I didn't want to think about, so I moved into position.

"Spread your knees wider," he said.

I was spread wide enough. He was ordering me wider simply because he could, to prove a point. But I did it; I widened my stance. If he wanted a show, he'd have one.

I was expecting to feel the foam right away, hoping it would hide the evidence of my arousal, but Syn stepped closer, sweeping two fingers over the wet lips of my pussy. I gasped, looking back at him. His eyes were on mine as he brought his fingers to his nose and inhaled, a slow smile spreading across his lips. His dark, clever eyes watched me watching him. And when he smeared those wet fingers on my hip, wiping them off, I was vanquished. My face burned and I did the only thing I could do. I faced forward and waited on my hands and knees, my back arched so that my bottom was thrust into the air, fully submissive, fully exposed to him as well as to the woman who would now shave me bare.

When it was over and I was instructed to rise, I did so quietly, not even sneaking a sideways glance at my captor. Without having to be told, I placed my hands at the back of my head and met the eyes of the other women who stood waiting for me, watching me as I had watched each one of them. Not a smile passed between us and I realized this shaving wasn't only done in order to bare us for our buyers, but to humiliate us, to let us know, as if there were any doubt left, that we were well and truly captives.

And I had a feeling this debasing was only the beginning.

※

SYN WATCHED THE GIRLS WALK QUIETLY AND IN A SINGLE FILE toward the flaps that made up the tent doors. They didn't need much instruction. The shaving always left them unable to speak. It worked well, and submission — even if under duress — was so much more rewarding than something taken with physical force.

Despite this, the weight of the cane in Syn's hand and the stripes on Eva's pretty little ass as she walked in front of him reminded him how enjoyable a less willing captive could be. Eva's arousal at the shaving told him one thing: even if her mind fought this, her body responded to it. She was a natural submissive. Intelligent and courageous, but submissive.

And honorable.

When she'd been given the opportunity to take the cane and punish the other girl as the girl had coldly punished her, she'd refused it. Syn wasn't sure he understood the purpose of such a notion anymore, but there was a time he had. Honor was something he once had had, wasn't it?

But thoughts of honor could be set aside. That was a long time ago and it had no place in his life anymore.

A guard opened the flaps of the tent and the girls walked out, stopping short when they took in the sight before them. Syn urged them forward with a tap of the cane against the first girl's hip.

Gabriel, who had remained outside of the tent, turned to them, looking the women over, his gaze resting on one in particular. Syn could see the look in Gabriel's eyes as he took in the slit of Evangeline's now bare pussy. They'd have plenty of time to see more of that shaved pussy though.

Now that they knew who she was, they had no choice but to keep her.

§

WE PAUSED WHEN WE STEPPED OUTSIDE. THE GIRLS WHO HAD yet to be shaved all stood with their backs turned to us, their legs at shoulder width, their hands still clasped at the backs of their heads. Gabriel stood nearby, watching us even as he spoke to one of the girls, his tone making it clear he was not pleased.

"Back in line, girls. Let's go," Syn said from behind me, the tap of his cane on my ass making me jump to attention.

"You six turn around. Go with Syn. You," Gabriel said, placing a hand on the back of a girl who already had a thick red welt across her ass and who was openly crying. "You'll take that dozen you're owed before getting your pussy shaved."

As he said it, two of the soldiers carried over the very stump I had knelt on and placed it a few feet from us.

Gabriel nodded his acknowledgement and tapped the girl's hip. "Kneel on the stump facing the others," he instructed, pointing to the stump.

I stood transfixed as I watched the scene, my body reacting so very differently than it should, my pussy absolutely throbbing as I watched her kneel on that stump and face us, reluctantly placing her hands at the back of her head, her hunted gaze sweeping over us as if looking for a rescuer. But no one spoke, the lot of us barely breathing — and not a single one of us came forward.

I remembered kneeling on that stump. Remembered the hard wood splintering into my knees. I remembered enduring the shame as I had assumed the same position she was now told to assume.

"Bend forward, hands on the ground and keep your face up. I want them to see you take your dozen. It will be good for motivation."

The stump was low enough that even with her hips lifted at this angle, she could easily look at us. For a moment, I felt grateful to Gabriel that he'd not made me do that. He'd not made me look at those who witnessed my humiliating punishment. And the fact that I was aroused at watching this now shamed me.

"A dozen. If you move, we start at one. Keep your face up, I want them to see you, understand?"

"Yes, sir."

"You'll all watch," he commanded the remaining group as Syn walked the others into the tent where Clara waited to shave them. "If anyone turns away, we start at one."

I noted first the thick, worn strap Gabriel held, then watched his face. His focus was wholly on the penitent before him. He shifted slightly to her side and placed a hand at her low back, bringing the strap to her ass to measure the stroke. The girl's whimpering grew louder when he did this, but I stood transfixed, able only to watch Gabriel's face. It was impassive, hard but not cruel as he raised the strap and brought it down across her vulnerable globes. My gaze then moved to her face as she gasped, tears welling in her blue eyes.

Lining up the next stroke, Gabriel struck again, then again. Each lash was timed precisely and as the spanking progressed, each stroke grew harder. I could see it from where I stood watching, could see the pain on the punished girl's face and wondered if that was how I had looked when I'd been birched or caned. I hadn't felt the strap yet but I had a feeling my bottom would become familiar with it soon. I glanced quickly at my companions who also watched, absolutely silent, and I wondered if they too found themselves aroused.

It was strange. When Syn had offered me the cane to punish Helena, no part of me wanted to take it. I would not, could not do this to someone, but the fact that watching it aroused me confused me, made me feel guilty for it. I shouldn't be enjoying another captive's pain and humiliation, should I?

Syn walked out of the tent with the group of girls, all of them now shaved as bare as the rest of us. One of them gasped when she saw the punished girl's buttocks.

Gabriel delivered the final strokes but forced the girl to remain as she was.

"Next time I tell you to bend over and spread your legs, what do you do?" he asked.

When she didn't reply right away, he fisted a handful of hair and lifted her head up. It was then that I saw the huge erection pressing at the front of his dark pants. He too was aroused. Aroused by strapping the girl. Was I the same as him then? Was I no better than my captors if I could become aroused by watching the pain and humiliation of another?

"I do as you say, sir," the punished girl said through tears.

"What's your name?" Gabriel asked her.

Syn stepped closer, apparently intent on having a look at his brother's handiwork.

"Monica, sir."

Syn moved behind her, the gazes of both brothers inspecting her intimately as Syn pulled one bottom cheek away from the other.

"You're wet, Monica," Gabriel announced.

Monica's eyes met mine then, her scarlet blush of shame flooding up from her neck to her face before she dropped her head.

Gabriel smiled and tapped her hip. "Get up," he said, helping her rise. "Punishment is over."

I found myself intently watching what happened next, part of me, unbelievably, waiting to see if Gabriel would hold her, if he'd let her cry on his shoulder like he had me.

It wasn't jealousy I was feeling, not quite, but a possessiveness I did not expect.

She stood on quaking legs and Syn took her by the arm into the tent to the waiting Clara. Gabriel's eyes were on mine when I turned back to him, but I didn't know how to describe what I felt in that moment. Was I glad that he'd not offered her the comfort he'd offered me? Yes. That, and relieved. Somehow, it felt special that he'd held me, comforted me after punishing me so cruelly.

Confusion dampened my arousal and for the first time in my life, I wondered who I was. I'd always been a good girl. I'd always done what I'd been told and I had always known what was expected of me, how I was to behave, first for my family, and then for Arthur. Emotions had never ruled me as completely as they did now, confusing me, as I tried to make sense of the missing revulsion I knew I *should* feel... a revulsion that was absolutely and undeniably absent. Who was I? In the space of mere days, had I become something other than what I'd been the past twenty years of my life? Was that even possible?

8

Gabriel told himself it was only the knowledge of who she really was that made him study her with even more interest now. He wasn't the only one keeping a closer eye on her either. He noted Syn's eyes on her and he needed to ask what had transpired in the tent between the women to earn Evangeline the three thin stripes across her bottom and Helena the dozen that decorated her plump cheeks.

But right now, he was only interested in Evangeline, in trying to understand what was going on in her head. The other girls stood wide-eyed, some teary, all frightened. All but Evangeline. It was as if a tornado was gathering in her pretty gray-green eyes. She'd watched him throughout Monica's punishment, but her gaze had grown even more intense afterward. He wondered if she'd felt aroused. She would be confused by that arousal if that were the case. After all, how could a civilized human being take pleasure in a fellow human being's suffering? Especially if that fellow human being was a captive, just like them.

Syn cleared his throat, drawing Gabriel out of his

thoughts. He checked his watch. The buyers would be here within the next hour. There was business to be done now. It wasn't the time to wonder about whether or not Evangeline was aroused by watching another girl punished. That time would come soon though. Soon, he and Syn would have the pretty girl home and all to themselves to study her intimately, to learn every one of her reactions.

"Are we addressing lying?" Syn asked quietly enough so that only Gabriel could hear.

Gabriel thought about it and glanced at Evangeline. He nodded.

"Tell me about obedience and disobedience, ladies."

There was just time enough for a collective intake of breath before they answered in one voice "Obedience is rewarded, disobedience punished."

"Good. Glad to see you are all understanding things." With that, he handed the strap back to a waiting guard and made a point of looking them all over. "You, up straighter. Get those tits out there. The more appealing you are, the more money you'll command — and tits appeal. That, and ass." He adjusted the girl and walked on to stand in front of Evangeline. Having the women shaved the way they had would have put them in the right frame of mind. What he'd ask next would drive that home. "You're all shaved bare at the front. I now need to see the back. Turn around, widen your stance to shoulder width and bend over, hands around your ankles, for inspection."

There were a few gasps and some of the girls began to cry.

Evangeline's face remained blank but her eyes met his directly. It wasn't defiance he saw in them, but curiosity. The mystery of her mind intrigued him, drew him to her.

"Move," Gabriel said. He was quickly running out of

patience with himself and would be glad to have the buyers come and take the women off his hands. He needed to keep a constant vigil over his thoughts, his actions. More than a dozen naked women parading around him, submitting to his commands, well, it was heady stuff, that power. It wasn't always easy to remain good, to do the right thing, at least in some ways.

The women turned, Evangeline along with them, but he called out her name to halt her.

"Evangeline. Not you."

She glanced at the women beside her, and he was glad to see that the look in her eyes was not one of relief at being singled out.

She was a smart girl.

"What's the hold-up girls?" Gabriel asked.

A moment later, he scanned the row of women, twelve of which were bent double, their legs wide enough that he could see between their cheeks, the pink lips of their pussies, the shadow of their darker back holes. Watching the girls assume so vulnerable, so exposing a position never failed to turn Gabriel's cock to steel. Only Evangeline remained standing, her hands clasped obediently at the back of her head, trepidation making her eyes dart from him to the women beside her, and back.

Gabriel adjusted his crotch.

"This will be your first inspection. This is also the position you will assume when your buyers want to have a look at you." Gabriel walked down the row of women, appreciating Clara's work. He didn't truly need to inspect anything but it was good for the girls to do this, to stand bent over, intimately and fully exposed. They would be made to feel vulnerable, and vulnerability went hand in hand with obedience.

He passed each woman, verbally adjusting a position once, twice, widening a stance. He didn't touch any of them though. Not until he came to stand in front of Evangeline.

"You lied to us," Gabriel said, pushing a stray hair behind her ear.

Evangeline trembled at his touch, her eyes widening infinitesimally. He might have missed the tiny change if he weren't watching her so closely. He could see the girls around Evangeline turn and look at her even from their bent positions.

"Lies won't be tolerated, and liars are punished."

"I don't know what you're talking about," she said, her gaze darting nervously to Syn who stood a few feet away, watching. She turned back to Gabriel, opened her mouth to speak, then closed it again, swallowing.

"I truly hope we're only ever going to have to do what we're about to do once, Evangeline."

"I didn't lie... I swear."

Syn clucked his tongue and shook his head. "That's two. I'm not really sure we've made any impression at all on our little Eva here, brother."

"It might appear you're right," Gabriel agreed, his eyes on Evangeline as he spoke to his brother. It was then that the guard brought over Gabriel's strap. He took it without looking away, noticing how her gaze flitted from him, to the strap and back.

Evangeline stepped backward, looking for a moment as if she would try to run, which would be ridiculous. She had to know that as well as he did.

"I didn't say you could take a step. Get back in line. Now."

She hesitated, glancing around her, but after a moment, she stepped back into the line.

"Where do your hands go?"

Her arms trembled as she raised them to interlace her fingers at the back of her head.

"Why did you lie to us about who you are?" Gabriel asked.

Distress marked her face when he tested the strap against his thigh as he asked the question.

"I... I didn't... lie..." She shook her head, her gaze faltering as it moved to the strap. It almost made Gabriel want to comfort her.

Almost.

But a lesson needed to be taught here and the truth needed to be determined.

"You're Senator Victor Webb's daughter. Arthur Gallaston's fiancée."

She stared up at him and he wondered if she thought he'd been bluffing all that time. "Please don't hurt me," she began, her voice low and oddly collected, almost calm. "I'm sorry. I didn't know what else to do." Her eyes reddened as tears welled, but she no longer denied having lied.

"What happened that he put you on that truck?" Gabriel asked.

At that, she seemed taken aback. "What?"

Gabriel looked her up and down. She was about 5'5" tall but petite in build. Her hair fell nearly to her waist, a pretty shade of auburn with strands of gold that picked up the sunlight as she moved, the thick bangs accenting her pretty, wide-set gray-green eyes. Her pale skin flushed easily and when her lip quivered, she bit it, her eyes pleading with him.

He thought of what Syn had said, how he'd never questioned if she was as innocent as she seemed. Some part of Gabriel wanted it to be true. He wanted to pull her into his arms, his instinct to protect as powerful as that to dominate. He realized then how the two went hand in hand, for him at least. Subconsciously or otherwise, once he'd learned the truth of who she was, he had decided that he and Syn would keep her for themselves.

It was more than that though. She'd had some strange effect on himself and his brother right from the start. He couldn't explain it exactly, but he never once doubted *how* she would be kept. He did not hide from his own dark nature, nor was he ashamed of it. Evangeline would be theirs to keep, to punish and to protect, depending, but she would be theirs.

If he believed in fate, perhaps understanding how things had happened would have been easier — but he didn't believe in fate. Neither that nor destiny. He believed in a world filled with cruelty which took from the innocent in as equal measure as the wicked, if not more. And as he looked on the face of the frightened girl, a strange anger crept along his thoughts, making him question what he was about to do. He knew where that anger stemmed from. He had felt it toward Laney too at one point, even as she'd lain there unconscious and helpless. Laney had put herself in harm's way. Had Evangeline done the same?

He forced himself to shift his thoughts to the man who carried the most guilt: Arthur Gallaston. What could have motivated the man to place his own fiancée on a truck to be sold like a piece of meat?

The hour for that evaluation would come later. Now was the time to learn the truth and to teach the girl before him a lesson.

"Over to the post, Evangeline. You're due a whipping."

Her eyes widened impossibly and she turned to look at

the lone post standing at the edge of the camp, a set of leather handcuffs hanging from the top.

"Please," she whispered, beginning to tremble.

He gestured to the post again.

"I was just afraid. I'm sorry, please don't do this." She touched her hand to the arm that held the strap, her voice dropping to a whisper. "Please don't punish me."

"I need some questions answered and I know one sure way to force the truth out of you. You'll be taking the strokes on your ass and thighs, unless you fight me. I'm giving you one chance to walk over to that post and surrender to your punishment. I can make you do it, easily, but if I have to do that, then I'll whip you from the tops of your shoulders down to the backs of your ankles before I start asking the questions. I can promise you, you do not want that, but I'll leave it up to you to decide. What's it going to be?"

She nodded miserably, placing both her hands behind her head. "Please." Tears fell from her eyes now as she physically shook. "I'm telling you the truth! I was just scared."

"As were the others, but you're the only one who lied. You have a choice to make. Are you walking or am I taking you to the post?" He wouldn't be swayed, not now, no matter how much his gut twisted inside him, telling him she was a victim, not a perpetrator of this crime.

He watched her throat work as she swallowed and she sent a pleading look to Syn. Was she hoping he would save her? Gabriel shook his head.

"Take her to the post," he said to a guard, his tone sharp.

The guard moved, but before he'd taken two steps, Evangeline jumped.

"No. I'll go. I'll walk. Please." She didn't wait, but turned and walked to the post. Gabriel halted the guard, taking in the sway of her hips as she moved, at the slight trembling of each cheek with every step. The lines from her birching had faded somewhat, but the three cane strokes still flushed a fresh red. He liked the look of it, of a woman's punished ass, and as much as he knew it was wrong, he knew himself well enough to admit he'd enjoy strapping her bottom now. And soon, he'd enjoy fucking it too. He'd already decided it would be him to claim her ass first. Syn would have her pussy.

※

Syn unlocked the cuffs on the post. He waited for her to come closer, watched her struggle to contain her tears. As hot as a woman's submission made him, Eva's vulnerability added an edge to that submission. It spoke to a different part of him, a part he'd managed to suppress for a very long time.

"Give me your hands, Eva," he said, keeping his tone gentle.

She held them out to him and he took them, turning them palms up to take in the delicacy of her small, pale wrists. Without thinking, he traced the fine blue line of a vein there.

So fragile, so... breakable.

He brought that wrist to his mouth and kissed it. Eva gasped but she didn't pull away. She couldn't have known his action surprised him as much as it did her, and when he returned his gaze to hers, he saw uncertainty in her eyes, that uncertainty momentarily overshadowing her fear for what was about to come.

She confused him, made him want to understand her, comprehend the workings of her mind.

And that confusion irritated him.

Annoyed at himself, he tugged her closer, raising her arms, wrapping a cuff around each wrist. Between the height of the post, and the shortness of the cuffs, she had to rise onto tiptoe.

Once she was secured, he stood back to observe his handiwork, taking in the lines of her body, her arms stretched up over her head, pulling her taut, the muscles of her back and shoulders tight, the small waist, the slightly wider hips and soft buttocks, perfectly proportioned legs, the muscles of her thighs and calves tensed.

Gabriel joined them and the determination Syn saw in his brother's eyes made him question what was about to happen. He wondered at the circumstances that had landed her here at camp. Had she been betrayed by her fiancé? Could Gabriel be right, that perhaps she was — or at one point had been — an accomplice? Everything inside him screamed no, screamed her innocence. But he knew his brother well enough to know he *needed* to do what he was about to do. He needed to do it to know for himself, even if Syn questioned if Eva even knew who was behind her kidnapping.

Gabriel moved into position and lined up the strap against her ass. Eva's wide-eyed, frightened face turned to look over her shoulder, her expression serving to harden Syn's cock, even though he doubted Gabriel's reasoning, doubted why she was about to be whipped.

"You're getting thirty for lying about who you are. We can stop there, or we can continue," Gabriel said, his eyes intent on hers as she craned her neck to look at him over her shoulder. "I'll ask you once before I begin. I don't know what you did that get you put on that truck, but I want to know if you were you a part of this, a part of Gallaston's organization?"

Syn watched her face, saw the confusion there. Her eyes flitted to his for a moment before Gabriel continued.

"Well?" Gabriel asked.

"I... I don't understand what you're asking me. I didn't do anything. I don't—"

Gabriel shook his head and cut her off. "I'll ask again after your thirty. Face forward, and think of what lying earns you. You'll count it out."

All was silent around camp, the eyes of the guards on them. Syn turned to the tent where the girls had been sent and saw them peering out from between the flaps, watching. The first stroke landed, the sound loud. A moment passed before Eva made any noise at all, her hands curling around the chain that held her cuffed wrists in place.

"Please!"

"The count, Evangeline," Gabriel said, laying on a second stroke.

"Two!"

The third stroke came, followed by the fourth and Eva began to dance around the pole, trying to avoid each one.

"Count or we start at one. And be still. Last time I'm reminding you."

"Four!"

She screamed when the next one landed and when she tried to dodge around the pole, Gabriel lowered the strap as Syn loosened his belt from his pants and stalked toward her. Grabbing hold of her arms, he moved her to stand where he'd first placed her with her back fully to Gabriel, and wrapped his belt around her waist, pulling it tight around her and the pole, securing her to it so she couldn't move more than an inch or two. He then looked at her, meeting her teary gaze with a tenderness he did not expect to feel. He wiped the moisture from her face with his thumb. "Be still and take it. You want this to end at thirty, understand?"

"Help me."

The unexpected words made Syn stop. He looked at her, at her reddened eyes, at the fear there, and something inside him shifted.

Help me. The words echoed in his head.

"Please, I'm begging you."

It took all he had to break eye contact and walk behind her to where his brother stood with the strap ready in his hand.

Gabriel nodded in thanks and picked up where he'd left off, landing three in quick succession. She cried out with each one, the numbers she spoke muffled by tears and begging.

Gabriel was laying into her hard, harder than Syn thought he would or should. He stood by and watched the next two strokes fall before speaking. "Easy," he said. "You'll break skin."

Gabriel looked at him, and in his eyes, Syn watched emotions collide. Gabriel's usual control was gone, replaced by a hot anger.

"Gabriel," Syn said, his tone brusque. He gripped Gabriel's forearm, halting the next stroke. "Give me the strap, let me finish it."

"No." Gabriel raised his arm, but Syn gripped harder.

"You don't want to do this, Gabe."

"I want the truth."

"And you already know it. She is here a prisoner, a victim, just like the others. You and I both know she had nothing to do with this. He chose it for her. Punish her for lying, but don't punish her for his sins."

Gabriel turned away, rubbing his hand over his mouth.

He took a deep breath in before turning his gaze back to the bound girl who whimpered quietly at the pole, her bottom already marked with thick, red welts. "Fuck." He handed the strap over to Syn and would have walked away, but Eva turned then to meet Gabriel's gaze.

"They're looking for me. If you know who I am then you know they'll find me, Arthur will find me. He won't stop." She began to cry and wiped her face against her arm.

"I wouldn't be too sure of that, Eva," Syn said, trying to end this before it began. Gabriel wasn't in a good place. He never lost his cool, not since what had happened to Laney. Eva was poking a bear she did not want to fuck with.

"He will. He loves me."

Gabriel stopped and took two steps back to stand directly in front of her. "No, honey." There was no warmth in the endearing term Gabriel used, even when he gently pushed the hair from her face. "He's the one who put you on that truck to be sold like an animal." His tone was angry, but his anger was misdirected. Gabriel must have known it too. He had to.

"That's not true," she said, her voice small.

"You don't know what your fiancé is capable of," Gabriel said.

"It's not true. You're lying. You're the liar!" she said more loudly.

"Enough, Gabriel!"

Gabriel shrugged Syn's hand from his shoulder, but remained silent, his eyes boring into the girl.

"Go, let me finish this." Syn watched Eva's face, her expression confused, hurt.

"It's very true and the sooner you realize that, the better off you'll be," Gabriel continued.

"I said *enough!*" Syn said loudly enough to make Gabriel

stop, to make him look at him instead of at Eva. "She doesn't deserve that." Then, so only Gabriel could hear: "She's innocent, like Laney was."

Gabriel glared at his brother, the wound of Laney's hopeless predicament as if still bleeding, still raw, still burning in his eyes. Tightening his lips, he glanced once more at Eva who stared at them from over her shoulder, her eyes widening. Without another word, he walked away.

Syn watched him, letting him go, shaking his head. He missed Laney too, missed the Laney he remembered, but there was a difference between himself and Gabriel. Gabriel carried the weight of what happened to her like a noose around his neck. As the eldest of the three, he'd always blamed himself for ever letting Laney get involved with drugs. By the time they'd found out how far gone she had been, it had been too late to save her. But Gabriel needed to remember that she was Syn's sister too. He loved her, felt her loss just as much as Gabriel did. Syn had just become more successful at shifting his focus, at funneling that anger, that hate.

He turned to the girl now bound to the stake and found her eyes on him, watching everything, seeing everything. Gallaston's sins did not belong to Eva. He would punish her for lying now, but he would not punish her for what was not hers.

"Face forward, let's finish this. I'll count."

She stared at him for a long moment, but turned to face forward.

Syn whipped her. He whipped her through her pleas, through her whimpers and screams, covering the flesh of her ass and thighs in angry crimson welts, delivering every one of the thirty his brother had promised the girl, taking her right to the edge but not beyond. Finally, it was done, and he handed the strap to a waiting guard, wiping the sweat from his forehead, turning to find Gabriel watching from behind the window of the RV, his expression closed.

"It's over," he said to Eva, collecting his belt from around her waist and looping it through his pants.

She whimpered quietly, hanging by her wrists, her weight supported by her restraints.

"I'll get you some water," he said, walking toward the RV.

"Wait."

He stopped, but didn't turn back.

"What he said, it's not true. It's not, is it?"

The last part of her sentence ended in a sob and he had the feeling she knew or at least suspected the truth, even if she couldn't yet face it.

He looked over his shoulder at her but couldn't bring himself to answer. He wouldn't lie. As much as truth could wound, Syn told the truth. Always. But this wasn't the time. Bidders would be arriving for the auction shortly. Once that was over and they could return home, then he would tell her. He would tell her all of it.

"I'll get you that water."

9

*A*rthur wouldn't have done this to me. Gabriel was lying — they both were. Out of the two of them, I'd thought Gabriel the more compassionate, the one just a little more human, but I was wrong. He was just as cruel, if not crueler, than his brother.

Syn had returned with a bottle of water and held it to my mouth while I drank it down, but he'd not said another word, and truthfully, I wasn't sure I wanted him to. There was one thing about the night I'd been taken that nagged at me but I couldn't think about that now. If I did, I might not be able to breathe.

I stood bound to that pole, my arms stretched so far above my head that I had to stand on tiptoe. I didn't know how long they'd make me stand here like this as the men of the camp ogled me, some standing behind me in pairs to discuss various details of my anatomy. Not a one of them touched me though and I knew I had the brothers to thank for that. Whenever I would glance at the RV they had disappeared into, I would see Syn's eyes on me, especially if there were men nearby. Somehow, I felt protected even from a distance, even by him.

The heat of the sun burnt my shoulders and I grew thirstier as the day wore on. I wondered if they'd contact my father now, ask a price and return me to him. I knew it was naïve to think it, but it comforted me, until I thought of the other girls, that is. I suspected the majority didn't have daddies with money to buy them back.

My gloomy thoughts were interrupted by the sound of approaching cars. I turned to watch the cloud of dust as several vehicles approached. Gabriel and Syn came out of the trailer, both casting a quick glance in my direction before turning to watch the motorcade.

"Get the girls. Line them up," Syn called out.

I heard commotion behind me as the women filed out. The vehicles came closer and my heart thundered in my chest, wondering what would happen to us now, to me. Wondering if and by whom I'd be bought. What that buyer would do to me.

When the first car came to a stop, Syn and Gabriel went to greet them. The other vehicles parked, one by one, and men piled out of each one — men and one woman. All had bodyguards with them and from the looks of them, out of the two dozen people, the woman appeared to be the most cruel as she scanned the group of women before bringing her gaze to rest on me, the scowl on her face turning into a smirk, her eyes narrowing into slits.

The buyers approached in a cluster, Syn and Gabriel leading the way, Syn talking to one while Gabriel wore his usual stern expression.

"This is a lovely sight to greet us, Gabriel. You've outdone yourself," the woman said, looking me over from head to toe, raising her eyebrows at my throbbing, hot bottom.

"Evangeline is troublesome," was all he said.

"I like a little trouble," the woman countered.

Gabriel glanced my way and I could see in his eyes that she bothered him. "Let her down," he said to one of the guards. "Take your place in line, Evangeline."

My heart raced. One of these men, or the woman, would buy me. I'd become a slave for the next three years of my life, if what the brothers said were true. If they really did intend to release us after that time. But why would they? Wouldn't we be a danger to them if they did? It didn't quite add up.

I didn't think of that though when a guard let me down. Instead, I rubbed my wrists and arms, trying to get the blood circulating again.

"Move," the guard said, gesturing to the line.

I watched as the other women stood neatly lined up, hands at the backs of their heads while the buyers looked them over, circling the naked women, evaluating, touching. It took a nudge from the guard before I joined the women in line, clasping my hands at the back of my head as I'd been told to do earlier.

Lara was crying already, as were several others whose names I did not remember. Something happened at the far end of the line and I turned to see Helena pushed to her knees while a man walked off toward a desk they had set up to the side.

Syn and Gabriel watched all of this, no one speaking but for murmurs. Asking questions, I presumed. When buyers began to circle me, I kept my gaze locked straight ahead. I would look at no one. I would feel nothing.

The woman came to stand before me, the weight of her

gaze demanding I meet it, but I refused. Why did I hate her more than I hated these men? Why did I find her more depraved?

"So you're troublesome," she said, lifting a breast, weighing it.

I swallowed, my lips tightening, my breath audible as I tried to hold my position. I knew what would happen to me if I didn't. Syn stood entirely too close with that cane at his side.

"I quite like troublesome." She walked around behind me. "My, my." Her fingernails scratched my buttock, making me suck in a breath.

"Bend over and touch your toes so I can have a better look here."

I obeyed. I don't know how, but I did. I bent forward, my fingertips brushing my bare toes. When the woman pulled my bottom cheeks apart and looked at me, looked at my most private places, all I felt was hate, a cold hate.

"When you're mine, I'll fuck you daily. Have you ever been fucked by a woman?"

I refused to answer, but when she smacked my hip hard with the flat of her hand, I stumbled forward, nearly falling.

"Myra," Gabriel called. "I have something special here for you."

"I'm quite enjoying something special right here, Gabriel."

I rose to stand, to watch what would happen.

"She's not for you." His tone made it sound final, even to me, and when I met his eyes, I felt something I didn't think was possible to feel after what had happened at that pole.

I felt Gabriel's protection.

He broke eye contact first, but not before I saw something that surprised me, something akin to guilt.

There was a moment of hesitation and I could feel a frustrated tension rolling off the woman.

"Shame," she said, then walked to where Gabriel stood. "Ah, but this one is lovely, isn't she. And seems more coy than that one there."

I looked at the girl who stood trembling before the woman, her eyes shiny with tears, her lip quivering. I should have felt relief that Gabriel had called the woman away from me, but I didn't. I felt hatred toward the horrible woman and fear for the girl she now appraised.

I straightened and a man came to stand before me, his breath fowl as he spoke to his bodyguard in a language I didn't understand. They walked around me, not once touching me, not yet.

"Open your mouth," he said in broken English.

I couldn't. I wouldn't. Even as I stood shaking all over, I couldn't do it.

"I said—"

"No, not that one." Syn's shadow fell over us.

I had never felt so relieved to hear Syn's voice or feel his cane at my thigh as I did in that moment.

"That one isn't for sale." Syn spoke quietly, his tone low, but there was no question he would be obeyed.

I met his dark gaze. The grin that turned up one corner of his mouth sent ice through my veins. He kept his obsidian eyes on mine when he tapped the cane against the front of my thigh once, twice, then, with a flick of his wrist, lashed me with it.

Tears stung my eyes as the rattan stung my flesh and I took a step backward, looking down at the welt rising where he'd struck. Thankfully, the man who had been considering me nodded with a reluctant growl before stepping to my right, to the next girl who stood shuddering beside me.

Gabriel joined Syn. Both brothers watched me intently as Gabriel whispered something into Syn's ear. Syn nodded, then turned his attention from me to the girl who was being handled by the prospective buyer. My gaze faltered when Gabriel approached and my body shook as he looked upon me.

"Evangeline," he said. "Kneel."

I understood now what it meant when a girl knelt. Once a girl was sold, she was made to kneel so that the next buyers knew who was still available. The girl beside me whimpered and I turned to see the large man weighing her breasts, turning her nipples in his fingers, his cock pressing against his pants as he fondled her.

"I'd like to try her," he said.

Syn's eyebrow went up. The girl stood upright, naked, her hands clasped at the back of her head. He looked her over, his gaze cold even as the girl now openly wept.

Syn turned back to the man. "You can look. You can even touch," he said, turning the girl so she stood with her back to the men. He then pushed her forward and down so she bent deeply at the waist. "But you can't *fuck* until you pay."

"Evangeline." Gabriel's fingers tightened in my hair, the girl's whimpers louder as he brought his mouth to my ear. "I said kneel. Eyes down. And just be glad it isn't you this time."

Without giving me time to obey, he forced me down by my hair until I knelt on the hard earth. I glared at him but my defiance lasted all of one second, the darkness I saw behind those beautiful golden eyes making me shudder. I cast my gaze to the ground before me, swallowing, shivering at what was to be my fate, knowing now that the brothers intended to keep me for themselves.

Gabriel glanced in the rear view mirror as he drove the pickup truck along the lonely road, leaving a trail of dust behind them. The girls had been sold within an hour, the fastest and most profitable shipment yet. Evangeline now sat in the enclosed back of the pickup truck, and Syn sat beside him. The RV had been driven off and a handful of guards had remained behind to break down the tents.

"What happened back there?" Syn asked.

Gabriel kept his eyes on the road. He knew what his brother referred to. He also knew he'd have to have this conversation.

"I don't know." He shook his head and turned to his brother. "I know she's innocent. God, I knew it then. I just… it was like I was punishing him when I had that strap in my hand. Fuck, Syn. I could have hurt her. Badly."

"You didn't."

"I could have." He looked at Syn. "Thank you for taking the strap from me." Gabriel wasn't sure himself what it was that had come over him when he'd been punishing Evangeline. He only knew that for a moment, for a very critical moment, he'd lost control. He'd let the anger he still felt over what had happened to Laney, the anger he blamed Arthur Gallaston and men like him for, to get the best of him, and he hadn't reigned himself in when that anger had turned on Evangeline. An innocent, helpless Evangeline bound to a post while he held the strap. "It won't happen again."

"I know it won't. She's not a part of Gallaston's organization. We know that."

Gabriel nodded, still angry with himself for having lost

control, for letting his own pain cause another innocent pain.

"What do you want to do about her?" Syn asked.

Gabriel shook his head. "Not sure. We can't send her back. He put her on that truck for a reason."

"I'm guessing the reason's money."

"Could be, but that can't be the only motivator. Her family is powerful, wealthy. Marrying her gives him access to that. Maybe he panicked? But why? Unless she figured something out."

"Can't be that. She believes he's looking for her."

"And he well may be."

"We'll have to make sure he doesn't find her."

"I don't plan on allowing that, brother," Gabriel said. "We'll keep her safe." Strangely, what had happened had bonded him to Evangeline in a powerful way. It was something he didn't expect and she did not know, but he meant what he said. She belonged to him now, to them, and she would be protected. "No way in hell I'm giving someone like him one more life to destroy."

"You aren't responsible for what happened to Laney."

Gabriel looked over at his brother. How many times had Syn said those words to him? How many times until he believed it?

Laney had been around Evangeline's age when she'd overdosed. Now, six years later, she lay in a special facility connected to too many tubes to count, brain-dead. If Gabriel had been around more, if he'd paid more attention, maybe he could have saved her.

But it was too late now.

"Let's get home. We'll talk to her, find out what exactly she knows and decide from there."

The next several hours passed in silence, each of the brothers lost in their own thoughts. Every time he'd peek into the back cabin, he'd find Evangeline sitting there staring out the window, her hands tucked between her knees, her bare feet turned inward, making her look even younger than she was. The sick bastard had loaded her onto a truck to be sold, knowing what her fate would be. Gabriel's hands fisted the steering wheel and his foot pushed harder on the accelerator. He wanted to get home, to change out of the dusty clothes he wore, have a shower and wash the filth from his body. Eat a decent meal. He and Syn had bought the home they lived in now and had it renovated three years ago. The place calmed him somehow. It was the untouched nature surrounding it as much as the gothic structure itself. It was secluded and remote, set on a large piece of land, sheltered from the world. It wasn't a house anyone would stumble upon by accident, so the rare guests they did have were ones they brought in themselves. Gabriel liked it that way. They both did.

"I hope Caroline cooked up some of her stew," Syn said. "I'm hungry."

"Me too."

Syn went over the numbers from the auction over the next half hour before, finally, they approached the tall gates to the old mansion. Gabriel punched in the code and they drove in. Two of the staff were out of the front door before they had even parked the car. Gabriel took one more look in the mirror at Evangeline who now stared around with wide, anxious eyes. He switched off the engine and stepped out.

"Thomas," Gabriel said, greeting the man who kept the house running when he and Syn were away on business. The number of staff were few: a cook, two cleaners and Thomas. All were paid exceptionally well and Thomas —

who knew everything about Syn and Gabriel's work — somehow kept it all under control.

"Sir. How was your business trip?"

Gabriel handed him the keys while Syn went around to get Evangeline.

"Excellent," Gabriel said. "How are things here?"

"Same."

Gabriel nodded. "You have a room prepared for our guest?"

Thomas looked at the truck where Syn helped their 'guest' out. "Yes, sir."

They'd had women here before, and between himself and Syn, they had particular tastes. Thomas didn't blink an eye and made sure none of the staff did either.

"Good. Tell your wife she'll have three very hungry people around the table for dinner."

"She'll like that. Caroline's made enough of her stew to feed twice that many."

Gabriel slapped Thomas on the back and smiled. It was good to be home.

"Thomas, this is our guest, Eva," Syn said, coming around with a very anxious Evangeline. "Eva, this is Thomas. He works for us but if you need anything, you'll ask Gabriel or myself first."

"Pleasure to meet you, madam," Thomas said.

She only stared.

"Say hello, Evangeline. It's rude otherwise," Gabriel instructed.

She looked at the older man, at the big house that loomed over them, cast in shadow as the sun began to set behind it, then turned to Thomas.

"Hello."

He could see her pulling back, resisting a little where

Syn held her, but that didn't matter now. She would do as she was told, as he and Syn decided, or she'd suffer the consequences.

Gabriel had no problem dishing out those consequences.

❧

I LOOKED AROUND AT THE LARGE HOUSE AS THE BROTHERS led me up the front stairs between them. They had introduced me to Thomas, a man who didn't seem at all bothered by my presence. Did he know what his employers did? Did he care? He had to know I wasn't a guest. I came barefoot and dusty, dressed in a dirty tunic, but he hadn't even blinked at my appearance. He'd simply taken the keys to the truck, said he'd make sure it was cleaned, and we'd walked away.

The large, gothic style mansion itself was pretty. The twin front doors stood open as we went inside. I looked around the foyer. I was used to wealth, I'd grown up surrounded by it, but this was something else entirely.

"Do you pay for this with the money you earn kidnapping and selling innocent women?" I asked when we stopped.

The brothers both looked at me.

"How do you think the house you live in is paid for?" Gabriel asked.

"Arthur doesn't do what you're suggesting. He wouldn't."

"You're wrong about that," Gabriel said. "Come on. You need a shower."

I hesitated but Gabriel gave my arm a tug and I moved down the hall toward the winding staircase. The scent of something delicious wafted out from what must have been the direction of the kitchen and my stomach rumbled loudly.

Syn smiled. "That's Caroline's stew."

Just as he said it, a door swung open and a portly older woman came through to greet us, wiping her hands on a towel as she did. The woman's eyes went wide for one moment when she saw me, but she recovered quickly. "Well, you boys are a sight. And you've brought a guest," she said, looking me over from head to toe.

"This is Evangeline, Caroline. She'll be staying with us for a while," Gabriel said.

"Well, it's nice to meet you, Evangeline. What a pretty name."

"Thank you, ma'am." Even at this first meeting, I knew there was steel behind the woman's polite façade. She was willing to overlook the fact that the way the brothers held me, I was clearly not a guest, not at all, and she didn't seem surprised, much less concerned.

"Stew is simmering. Get cleaned up and I'll get the table set for dinner. I don't want you tracking that dust all over the house."

"No, ma'am, wouldn't think of it. But we'll be quick. I've missed your food, Caroline." Syn said.

Caroline nodded, smiling proudly, and turned to go back toward the kitchen. We continued up the stairs and to the second floor where the hallway led away in two directions. Doors lined the corridor, the double doors at either end presumably leading to master suites.

"Here we are," Syn said at the third door we passed. "Your room."

"I don't need a room. I want to go home."

Gabriel's cell phone rang then and he looked at the display. "You got this?" he asked Syn.

Syn nodded, looking like he couldn't be happier. "In you go," he said to me.

I held on to the doorframe, feeling somehow more desperate now than I had at the camp. "I said I don't need a room. I want to go home."

The flat of his hand landed hard against my bottom and I gasped, reaching back to cover myself.

"Ow!"

He smiled. "In, Eva."

Although reluctant, I stepped inside, scanning the room. It was pretty, remarkably so. I wasn't sure what I'd expected, but the room was large, more of a suite, with a four-poster king size bed in the center, heavy drapes along each of the three windows, and a rich carpet covering the floor, all in shades of blue.

"Bathroom is here," he said, closing the door behind us.

I followed him into the luxurious bathroom, which was a spacious room in itself. A gorgeous creamy marble covered the walls and floor, and a large, old-fashioned tub with feet stood at the center. Along one wall was the large walk in shower and two double sinks along the other. The toilet was in a separate space.

"Did you expect we'd keep you in a barn?" he asked.

I turned to find him stripping off his shirt. "What are you doing?"

"Taking off my clothes so I can have a shower. You should do the same."

I shook my head and went to exit the bathroom, but he closed the door before I reached it, his hand resting against it over my head.

I turned to face him.

"Get undressed, Eva."

I shook my head again, looking up at him, feeling small. He topped me by more than a head.

He stripped off his shirt to reveal his tanned, wide shoulders, muscular chest, arms and abs. I found myself staring at his physique, unable not to. Arthur didn't look like this. No one I'd ever seen in real life looked like this. Not that I'd been with many men. Arthur was it, actually.

"Take off your dress, Eva. I've seen you naked before. I've seen every intimate inch of you and I plan on seeing it much, much more often. But if you'd rather make it difficult, I don't mind making you, you know that."

He unzipped his dark jeans and took them down over his hips, then did the same with his underwear. I swallowed, my eyes widening at the strip of dark hair that trailed down from his belly button to the thicker mass of it just above his thick and very erect cock.

When I saw that, I turned my face, covering it with my hands.

Syn laughed. "You have seen a man's cock before, haven't you?"

"I don't want to see yours. I want to go home," I cried from behind my hands.

"This is home now. The sooner you accept that, the better things will go for you."

His tone was serious and I looked through my fingers to find him switching on the shower, testing the water temperature, but all I could look at was his powerful back, muscled legs and tight buttocks.

He turned to me. "We'll talk about how you got on that truck to begin with once we get downstairs. But for now, I'm going to need you to strip off your clothes and get in the shower. I'm hungry, Eva, but if you need me to punish you first, I can do that."

"You go first. I'll have one when you're done," I tried.

"I don't think so."

He took a step toward me and I took one back, my body pressing against the door, my eyes locked on his thick, hard cock.

"I'm not going to hurt you," he said more softly, understanding my hesitation.

I looked up at him.

"I want to go home. Please." Tears felt hot behind my eyes. I knew I was trapped. I knew I was a prisoner. But in a way, I didn't realize how completely powerless I was until this moment. He could make me to do anything he wanted me to do. Although I didn't know where I was exactly, I knew we were far from civilization. I had seen the street signs change from English to Spanish and knew we'd crossed the American/Mexican border without having to stop. The staff of the house I'd met didn't blink an eye at seeing me here in the state I was in. What did that say? That it wasn't their first time having someone here like this? Home seemed farther and farther away, like months had passed since I'd been there even though I knew it had only been days, and I felt hopeless.

Syn stepped closer and rubbed his hands over my arms.

I covered my face, not wanting to cry.

"Look at me, Eva."

I shook my head.

"Look at me."

He forced my hands off my face and I looked up at him. "This is your home now. This is where you'll be for the time being. Do you remember what we said at camp? Just before you were made an example of?"

I nodded. I remembered that well.

"Same goes here. Obedience is rewarded, disobedience

punished. Now are you stripping off your clothes and getting into the shower or am I going to have to punish you first?"

I didn't want to be punished. What I wanted was to have that hot shower and eat whatever it was I smelled downstairs before going to bed. I wanted to sleep and when I woke up, I wanted to find that this had all been just a bad dream.

I knew it was impossible, but I wanted it anyway.

Syn watched her as she pulled the dress over her head, dropping it to the floor. He gestured to the shower and she walked ahead of him, opening the door and stepping inside. He followed her in, and, without hesitating, pulled her to him, her back against his hard chest, and held her until she relaxed. Water flowed over them and he heard the faint sounds of her crying.

Her skin was soft, slippery from the water, and his cock ached to have her so close and not claim her.

"You're very pretty, Eva," he said, his hands moving to cup her breasts, the nipples hardening in his palms.

She gasped but didn't pull away and he slipped his hand lower, his fingers separating to touch the space on either side of her slit before moving back up. With his other hand, he took the bottle of shampoo and poured some out onto his palm. She didn't hesitate when he began to massage the stuff into her scalp, working it into a lather before guiding her head below the stream of water. Once the suds washed off, he repeated the process before pouring body wash over his palm and beginning to rub it over her body.

"You'll have to get used to us doing everything for you

now," he whispered into her ear as he massaged her shoulders, her arms, each of her hands. Her breasts were next and he took his time, kneading each one, turning the nipples softly, then with a little more pressure until he heard her gasp of breath and her hips pushed back against him. He wondered if she was aware of that slight movement, and while one hand teased her breast, the other slid down between her legs.

"Oh..."

"Open your legs wider so I can clean you, Eva," he whispered, his cock a spike against her back now.

She obeyed and when his hand cupped her sex, she moaned soft and low.

"That's it, just like that." His other hand left her breast and came down behind her, over the side of her hip and toward the cleft of her buttocks. "I have to clean you here too." Without hesitating, he slid his finger between her bottom cheeks, the soapy digits finding her back entrance.

"Oh... please..."

She reached out with both hands to brace herself against the walls and leaned her head into the crook of his shoulder.

"Obedience is rewarded," he whispered into her ear, rubbing her pussy harder, paying special attention to her swollen nub as other fingers circled her back hole, until she was pressing her hips into him, her breath coming in gasps. When he took her clit between thumb and forefinger, she cried out and he had to hold her tight to him as her knees gave way and she came, her body going limp in his arms, her orgasm causing her to make the sweetest little sounds he'd ever heard

10

"You took your time," Gabriel said. He folded the paper he'd been reading and set it down on the dining room table, looking up to find his brother bringing Evangeline in. Her step was soft and her expression confused but curious, and obviously compliant as she walked with Syn's hand at her back rather than wrapped around her arm. He had an idea how his brother had helped her to relax while washing her and smirked at Syn when he seated Evangeline at the table, noting the tight stretching at the front of his brother's pants.

"You must be hungry," he said, turning to Evangeline, touching her hand lightly as Syn took his place at the square table.

She looked from Syn to him and nodded.

"I don't have clothes," she said, sounding like a lost little girl.

"No, you don't. Clothes are a privilege here, not a right."

"I don't understand any of this. I don't…"

"Ah, well, now that's better, isn't it?" Caroline said, walking into the dining room followed by two younger girls.

She carried the pot of stew and set it at the center of the table.

Gabriel watched Evangeline throughout, saw her face brighten to a pretty crimson at the quick, curious glances from the girls. Caroline kept her staff in check though. You wouldn't know it from looking at the sweet older woman, but she kept her own cane in the kitchen should any of the staff prove problematic. They rarely did.

"Smells delicious," Syn said.

"Thank you," Evangeline's small voice came when her bowl was filled.

"Arms at your sides, Evangeline. You're never to cover yourself," Gabriel said.

She looked at him, a thousand questions in her eyes, then bowed her head, obeying, no longer covering her breasts.

"Enjoy," Caroline said before she and the two girls left the dining room.

"Go ahead, Evangeline," Gabriel said when she hesitated. She looked over at Syn as if for confirmation, but he simply ate. She had become more afraid of Gabriel than of Syn over the last day or so. He could understand it. What had happened at camp when he'd punished her weighed on him, but she'd learn soon enough though that both brothers punished and both pleasured equally.

"Delicious," Syn said, setting his spoon down and breaking apart a piece of bread. "Would you pass the butter, Eva?"

Gabriel took it all in, noticing how she'd barely sipped her stew. She set her spoon down and passed the butter dish to his brother.

"Nice shower?" Gabriel asked her.

She looked at Syn who merely glanced back at her.

Theirs To Take

"Yes," she answered quietly.

"Yes, what?"

"Yes, sir."

"Eat, Evangeline. Don't be ashamed of your nakedness."

"She comes beautifully," Syn said the moment she had put a spoonful into her mouth, causing her to splutter on the stew.

"I can't wait to see for myself," Gabriel said.

"I left your preferred area unpenetrated."

"Please!" Evangeline called out, dropping her spoon with a clang against her bowl, splashing stew over the white tablecloth.

Gabriel looked at it, then at her. "Manners, Evangeline. You'll have to be taught them I suppose."

"I don't understand." She covered her face and began to cry. "I want to go home. Please let me go home. My father will pay. Please. I won't say anything about what happened or about you, I promise."

Gabriel reached over and laid a hand on her shoulder. "We'll talk after you eat. We'll get everything sorted out once you've finished. We're not here to hurt you, in fact, you're as safe as you can be with us. But I don't like talking to someone who isn't listening." He paused. "Are you listening?"

She kept silent, her hands still covering her face.

"If you're going to act like a child, I am going to treat you like one. Now tell me, are you listening or do you need me to take you over my knee and spank you first to make you listen?"

At that, she pulled her hands away and glared at him.

"Better. In the future that sort of behavior will earn punishment, but for now, I'll be lenient, given the circumstances. Pick up your spoon and eat, please."

Without a word, she did as she was told and ate her bowl of stew. Once she took that first bite in fact, she finished it faster than either of the brothers did, and sat pointedly eyeing the bowl at the center of the table.

"Would you like more?" Gabriel asked.

"Yes, please."

Gabriel stood and served her a second bowl of the rich stew and Syn handed her a buttered roll. She took it and ate the second serving, this time a little more slowly.

"Have you eaten enough?" Gabriel asked her when she sat back, her hand on her belly.

"Yes. It was delicious."

"I'm glad. Let's go into the library to talk."

He stood, waiting for her to do the same, and with a hand at her back, guided her to the library.

※

I WAS NAKED. EVERYONE AROUND ME WAS DRESSED AND I WAS naked. It didn't even seem to matter to anyone that this was the case. My hands were at my back covering my bottom as best as I could while I walked, but I could feel their eyes on me, on my bottom. It was embarrassing to say the least. It put me on a different level from them.

The library was the last room down a long hallway. When Gabriel opened the tall doors to let me in, I paused, taking it all in. It was a big room with high ceilings and one of the walls was rounded rather than straight and made up entirely of iron-framed glass windows that arched from floor to ceiling. It was magnificent. Breathtaking.

"Go on," Gabriel said, pressing gently at my back.

I stepped in and turned a circle, feeling like a child as I stared up at the stacks and stacks of books, many of which

I'd have to use the ladder to get to. Two heavy, antique desks stood at opposite ends of the room and a large stone fireplace at another. The floor was covered with a rich, deep red carpet and large, worn leather chairs and two ottomans made up the furnishings.

When I was finished looking around, I turned back to find both Gabriel and Syn watching me. Looking at Syn made me blush, the memory of what he had done to me in the shower, at what I'd not even pretended to resist, still too fresh. And I had no doubt he was enjoying my discomfort.

"You may kneel here, Evangeline," Gabriel said, pointing to a spot before two of the armchairs.

"Kneel?"

He gave me a sideways smile while they assumed their seats and I sat on my heels, facing them. If they wanted me to know my place, I already knew it. This was unnecessary.

"Hands on your thighs, palms turned up, Eva," Syn said.

I followed his instruction, noticing how he called me Eva and Gabriel always called me by my full name.

"Let's lay everything out on the table so we're all on the same page here, Evangeline. We know who you are, your father and fiancé were on the news begging for your safe return. Or at least your father was. Gallaston was doing a half-assed job pretending to."

"Why do you keep saying that? Why do you hate Arthur?" A heavy weight settled in my belly as I asked the question, the same anxiousness I felt every time Arthur's name was brought up.

"Can you tell us what you remember about the night you were kidnapped?" Syn asked.

"How long ago was that?"

"Just a few days. Tell us what you remember."

"We were in Scottsdale for a fundraiser, it happened on

the night of the event, shortly after it was over. I was tired and Arthur and I had had a fight earlier. We'd been fighting more and more lately. I thought he might have been having an affair," I admitted for the first time. I glanced at my captors when I did, but what I saw in their eyes wasn't concern. They remained studying me intently, waiting for my next words as if they weren't surprised at all by what I had just said. I lowered my gaze to my lap.

"Go on."

"He wasn't though. I know that but I don't know how I know. Why can't I remember?"

"They most likely used a sort of date rape drug on you when they kidnapped you. You wouldn't have any memory of the events after that was injected. And I'm wondering if the bump on your head has something to do with why you can't remember much previous to it," Gabriel said.

"That or she's blocking it," Syn added.

"Also a possibility."

"Why do you say he wasn't having an affair? Why did you suspect it but no longer do?" Syn asked.

"I don't know why. I just know he wasn't." That weight in my belly was back and I shivered. Syn got up, retrieved a throw blanket folded on top of one of the ottomans and draped it over my shoulders. My fingers touched his as I took it and I looked up at him. "Thank you."

He merely nodded and resumed his seat while Gabriel continued with the interrogation.

"What did you fight about?" Gabriel asked.

"Nothing. Well, I don't know. We'd been fighting more lately. He was under a lot of pressure. I should have known that and listened to him."

Gabriel glanced at Syn whose eyebrows went up.

"None of this would have happened then."

"What do you mean?"

I shook my head, rubbing my temples and squeezing my eyes shut. This was so frustrating, I just wanted to remember! "I don't know! And I'm getting a headache thinking about it."

The brothers waited quietly for me to continue and I took a deep breath to force myself to go on.

"Arthur got a call at the fundraiser and he hadn't looked happy about it. It changed his whole mood. Things were getting heated, I could hear it from where I sat beside him, and he'd had to excuse himself from our dinner table. When he wasn't back a few minutes later, I went out to find him." I paused, remembering what had happened.

"Where was he?"

"He wasn't on the phone anymore. He was talking to someone in person. Someone I had never seen before, someone I couldn't imagine him knowing. He was angry, and it's rare for Arthur to get so upset. He's usually very much in control of... well, of everything."

"Go on."

"Jamison was there. He was always there. Jamison worked with Arthur long before I knew him. Arthur trusted him and he didn't trust many people."

Syn nodded at me to continue while Gabriel remained studying me.

"They were talking about a shipment. About needing more money. Arthur said he'd have it soon. That was when I'd tripped over something and had gotten his attention. He'd snapped at me. He'd never done that before. For the first time ever, I'd felt frightened of him. It was something about the look in his eyes. He was so... so angry. It was a side of him I didn't know."

"Can you describe the man he was talking to?"

I shook my head. "He stepped into the shadows when he saw me and I didn't get a good look. Another couple walked out of the banquet hall and Arthur composed himself quickly, put on the face I knew well and led me back inside." I then asked the question that had been on my mind since the start of this. "What do you plan to do with me?"

Gabriel ignored the question and went on. "The night you were kidnapped, Gallaston claimed you'd gone out for a jog and he didn't realize you were missing until the next morning."

"What?" Were they lying to me? Why would Arthur have said that? He knew it wasn't true. I rarely went running and if I did go, it was with a friend early in the morning.

"That's what he told the police."

I looked from one to the other, trying to understand. Was everything I knew a lie? "Please don't lie to me about this. I'm here. You have me here." Confusion boiled up inside me, building like a volcano, that layer of dread at the thought of Arthur churning hot within it. "I don't understand. Please don't lie to me." I felt desperate.

"That's one thing we won't do, Eva. We will always tell you the truth."

I looked into Syn's eyes, his black, black eyes, and I knew what he said was true. I believed him.

"Arthur knew I wasn't going for a jog. I wouldn't have, it was so late. He had told me to go to our room saying he'd be up soon." I looked up at Gabriel. "But I didn't go. I followed him instead. I remember that, I followed him."

"What else, Evangeline? Think."

I *was* thinking. I was thinking so hard it hurt. I looked down at my left hand, at the thin white line where my engagement ring should have been. But I didn't want to think about that now. I couldn't think about that.

"What's going to happen to me?" I knew my memory of that night was critical, but I also knew it would answer more questions than I wanted answered. Than I could handle having answered.

Syn looked to Gabriel and nodded, and Gabriel turned back to me.

"I know you don't want to believe this, Evangeline, but your fiancé has been trafficking women for years and is heavily involved in moving drugs throughout the United States."

I shook my head. This was... unreal.

"Your father is offering to pay a hefty amount of money to anyone with information about you."

"You can tip him off anonymously. Drop me somewhere. Tell him where to find me. Make some arrangement to get paid."

Syn frowned. "Look around you, Eva. Does it look like this is about money to us?"

I shook my head. "What is it about then?"

Syn got up, opened a desk drawer and brought back a photograph. "This was Laney. She was barely twenty-one when she overdosed on drugs."

I looked at the girl in the picture standing between Gabriel and Syn. The resemblance between them was uncanny.

"I... I'm sorry, that's terrible." It *was* terrible, but why were they telling me this? "Did she..."

"No, she didn't die, but she was pronounced brain-dead. She's in a vegetative state, has been for six years."

"I'm sorry, but I don't understand what this has to do with me."

"She got involved with a man like your fiancé," Gabriel

said. "She'd never even smoked a cigarette before him. Laney didn't do drugs."

I didn't know what to say.

"She was pregnant. We found that out later, once she'd miscarried."

I just sat watching, horrified, not knowing what to say, how to even react.

"The night before they'd found her lying on the street, like some animal — she'd left a phone message," Gabriel said, continuing to talk. "I didn't get to hear it until it was too late." He stood and went to his desk, taking out a cell phone and pushing a button. I didn't want to hear it but I had no choice. Turning to him, I watched his face as I listened, watched him try to contain the hurt, saw his hand clench to a fist as the message played. She spoke in a near whisper, her voice sounding anxious and afraid.

"I want to come home, Gabe, but I'm not sure he'll let me leave." A nervous giggle then she began to whisper. *"I sound stupid, don't I? I mean he's my boyfriend."*

Laney gasped, a door slammed shut and someone called out her name.

"I have to go. I'll..."

The call ended there, just like that.

"Those were her last words to us," Syn said, but my eyes remained on Gabriel who looked at the phone for a moment before putting it away, averting his gaze from mine.

Gabriel leaned against his desk and folded his arms across his chest, watching me. "You want to know what's going to happen to you? I'm not convinced putting you within Gallaston's reach is the safest thing for you."

"He wouldn't hurt me! He didn't do this to me." But he'd lied about my having gone for a run that night. Why would he have done that? Had he lied then or was I being lied to now?

I rubbed my face, my tired eyes, trying to understand.

"If we let you go, you could cost us everything."

"I won't! I promise. I just want to go home."

There was a long pause and I knew the questioning was over, and as much as I'd wanted them to stop, this change made my heart beat pick up.

"What if I said I didn't *want* to let you go, Evangeline?" Gabriel asked, his words suddenly cool, calculating, his eyes scanning my naked body. "What if I said I wanted to keep you here?"

I could only stare up at him.

"Stand up."

I looked over at Syn who stood watching me, his eyes unreadable.

"I said, stand up," Gabriel repeated, his tone unchanged.

From the corner of my eye, I saw Syn rise and walk to the door before I heard the lock turn.

"Evangeline."

Every hair on my body stood on end, ever muscle tensing, almost vibrating in trepidation. I shook my head, unable to speak.

"Time for that inspection you missed earlier," Gabriel said, opening a drawer and taking out a strap similar to the one he'd had at camp, the one I'd been whipped with.

"No..." I began to rise, but paused, kneeling up instead.

He set the trap on the desk. "Besides, my brother and I always share our women and he's had a sampling. It's my turn," Gabriel said.

"She was sweet," Syn said. "Soft and... willing."

"No. Please don't."

Syn returned to stand behind the chair he'd earlier occupied, leaning on the back of it, watching me.

"I haven't taken you over my knee yet," Gabriel said. "Haven't felt with my bare hand how you take a spanking. Maybe it's time to remedy that."

I could only watch as he approached, resuming his seat on the armchair but leaning in close so that our faces were inches apart. I pulled back, letting the blanket slide to the floor, his closeness unnerving me.

"Over my lap, Evangeline. We'll start there."

Swallowing was difficult, the lump in my throat too big. Tears wanted to fall but I wouldn't allow them, no matter how afraid I was.

"Or do I need to make you?" he asked, looking a little too enthusiastic.

Before I could process what he'd said, he took hold of my arm, his grip painful as he hauled me upward. My hands went to his knees as I tried to push back and free myself, screaming when he easily pulled me up and over his knee, catching my right wrist in his hand, the positioning of my body tight against his. He forced my left hand to remain on the floor as he adjusted my position, shifting his legs and trapping mine between his, my head hanging low, my bottom now the highest part of me.

"Let me go!" Even knowing how useless any pleading or struggling would be, I carried on while he said something to Syn who stood back watching, the two of them talking almost calmly while I flailed around on Gabriel's lap, trying to free myself.

"I know you were wet watching the other girls get shaved," Gabriel said, the hand that had been rubbing circles on my bottom now rising and falling hard against my still tender flesh, causing me to cry out. "And I wonder if you weren't also wet watching the girl get strapped." Another hard spank left me breathless. "I think," he continued spanking me as he spoke, one cheek, then the next, then back again, not a moment between smacks for me to catch my breath. "You might even enjoy submitting to us more than you know, more than you're willing to admit. That's always a difficulty with women."

"At least at the start," Syn added.

I looked back to find him standing off to the side, watching while Gabriel spanked me.

"Please. It hurts!" Although it didn't hurt as much as the punishments at camp had, being over his lap like that and him using his hand was different somehow.

"Not yet it doesn't," Gabriel answered me. "She does turn a pretty pink quickly."

"Too bad she's already striped from this afternoon's whipping," Syn said. They spoke as if I wasn't there at all. "You're taking it easier on her than I'd expect otherwise."

"I'm not sure she thinks that."

"I hate you. I hate you both!" Tears fell from my eyes and I had to use my free hand to wipe my face, wiggling my bottom to escape the spanking that came harder and faster now, three to a cheek in the same spot before he moved to the other side and repeated. The sting was terrible, and my skin felt dry and stretched, but he kept on spanking, talking to his brother or to me, I wasn't sure anymore. All I could think about now was the pain and, in a way, being wholly absorbed by so physical a thing as that punishment was what I needed to block everything else out.

I stopped begging him to stop then, stopped fighting altogether and allowed myself to go limp over his lap. I wept. I wept like I couldn't remember ever weeping before, not holding back, snot and tears running down my face while he kept spanking me, the two of them no longer speaking, until I was too exhausted even to cry, every tear in me spent. While my bottom throbbed hot, my belly felt soft, that weight, that dread I'd been feeling since I woke up in that truck gone for the first time.

"There," he said quietly. "I think you needed that."

I had neither the strength nor the desire to fight as he gently lifted me into his arms and held me on his lap. I tried to bow my head against his chest, not wanting him to see me like this, ashamed and exhausted at once, but he wouldn't let me. Taking the tissues Syn handed him, Gabriel cleaned my face, pushing away the hair plastered to my wet cheeks, forcing me to look up at him, to meet his gaze. His eyes had darkened, the pupils dilated, and I realized what it was that pressed against my thigh. I looked at his mouth, his full lips, and in that moment, after all that had happened, all I wanted was for him to hold me, to kiss me, to make everything else go away.

Caught up in the mix of emotions, the confusion, this unfamiliar need to be held, comforted, I leaned in to kiss him, the look in his eyes at first surprised, then pleased. He denied me that kiss though and instead righted me, making me stand up between his legs, his hands around my wrists preventing me from rubbing my throbbing bottom. I looked down at him as a single tear rolled down my cheek. His eyes were stern, serious. There was no humor in them. He held me like that and I realized I'd calmed somewhat, the stinging pain across my backside receding into a throbbing heat that I didn't altogether hate.

I looked at Gabriel's mouth, desire once more building inside me, awakening parts of me I never imagined would respond to something like this. My exhaustion gone, I wanted one thing. I wanted his mouth on me, on my mouth, on my breasts, on my sex. It was as if he were waiting for me to come to that realization and once I did, I watched his gaze slide down to my breasts, to the peaked nipples. He tugged on my wrists, forcing me to lean closer, and with his eyes on mine, he opened his mouth and took one nipple into his mouth.

I gasped, the soft heat of his mouth not what I expected. But he held me as I was, watching my eyes as he sucked on the pebbled peak before drawing it out with his teeth, the sensation just this side of pleasure. When he released it, my breath grew ragged, the air cool against my nipple as he turned his attention to the other one, taking it into his mouth and repeating what he'd done with the first.

Fingers at my bottom reminded me there were three of us here. While Gabriel sucked on my breasts, Syn scratched fingernails down over my freshly spanked bottom before gripping the fleshiest part of my buttocks and spreading them open, holding me like that so that the air in the room felt cool against my wet sex, my bottom.

"Sweet like honey," he said from close behind me before he knelt and Gabriel released my breast, pulling me even more forward so that I was bent over, my ass pushed out behind me, Gabriel's eyes on mine.

A whimper of pleasure, of anticipation, of resistance — I wasn't sure which — came from me when Syn's hands spread my bottom cheeks wider and I felt his tongue at the entrance of my sex.

"Oh..."

Gabriel wrapped his hands around my arms, holding me in position, as, while his brother tasted my pussy, he tasted my mouth. I opened for him, my eyes closing, the sensation of Syn's tongue licking my pussy, tickling my clit and the softness of Gabriel's kiss contrasting so completely with the hot throbbing of my spanked bottom.

"She is so sweet," Syn said from behind me, the work of his clever tongue stopping too soon. I found myself shamelessly pushing backward, wanting him there, wanting his mouth on me.

Gabriel stopped kissing me, his eyes on mine as he released me altogether and I could do nothing but stare into their golden depths. When I stumbled backward, Syn caught me by the shoulders, steadying me. He held me in place while Gabriel sat back in his chair. But I didn't need to be held. I wouldn't have run, not now. Gabriel's gaze moved to my belly, my slit.

"Spread your legs wider," he said. "Show me your pussy, Evangeline."

I did, not wanting to want this, wishing my body would obey that part of my mind that told me to fight. But I didn't want to fight.

"Where do your hands go during inspection?" he asked, looking back up at me.

I didn't reply with words. Instead, I raised my arms and clasped my hands at the back of my head.

He nodded his approval, then returned his attention to my pussy, two fingers coming to touch my mound.

"We'll keep your pussy bare going forward."

His thumb pushed on the side of one lip, exposing me to him.

"Put your foot on the arm of the chair, Eva. Show my brother your pretty little cunt," Syn said. It didn't occur to me to disobey, and as obscene as I knew I would look when I did it, I raised one leg up, resting the foot on the arm of the chair Gabriel occupied.

"Good girl," Syn said from behind me.

"Obedience is rewarded," Gabriel said, his hands coming to either hip, pulling me toward his face until he could take the swollen, exposed nub of my clit into his mouth and suck, his eyes on me as he did.

"Oh...God!"

I reached to catch Gabriel's shoulders and would have collapsed but for Syn catching me. He held my arms behind my back, my wrists together in one of his hands, his body pressed against me, my head reclining against his shoulder.

"Oh... please..."

Gabriel sucked harder, sliding one finger into my pussy, and as he did, Syn turned my face to the side, kissing my mouth deeply, his tongue tasting me, devouring me. When I came and my knees gave out from under me, the brothers supported me, their lips upon mine, still kissing, sucking, taking, giving until I shuddered with orgasm. My juices spilled over Gabriel's tongue as I let out a long, trembling moan.

Unable take any more, I collapsed on my knees before him, my head in his lap, his hand coming to the back of it, caressing my hair gently, the brothers speaking quietly, their voices muted as I drifted off to sleep.

11

"She's definitely blocking," Syn said, standing over Eva. She had fallen asleep in Gabriel's arms and hadn't woken when he had lifted her to carry her to her bed.

"I agree. She should remember up until they injected her." Gabriel turned her head slightly to touch the faint bruising still visible at her neck and forehead. "And they weren't gentle."

"She must have surprised them."

"That's what it sounds like. Gallaston was anxious, she'd said."

"Look at these," Syn ran soft fingers over scrapes and cuts along her body. "And her dress was torn and filthy."

"Well, we can't send her back to him. He'll finish the job if we do."

"But her father's a prominent politician. It doesn't make sense. Too much press."

"He's desperate," Gabriel said, standing.

Syn tucked the covers up over her shoulders. "Which makes him weak."

The brothers walked to the door, and, after one more

glance at their sleeping captive, switched off the light and left her bedroom.

※

I KNEW IT WAS A DREAM, OR RATHER, A NIGHTMARE, BUT I also knew it was very real. At least it had been once. Arthur and I were dancing. I was wearing my pretty new dress, the one he'd insisted on buying me even though it was well over our budget.

But it was ruined already.

Arthur stood impeccable in his tuxedo while I walked barefoot, having lost my shoes under the bridge. Oily dark blotches covered my dress and the silk was torn in places. I looked at my arms, at my hands, which Arthur held as he twirled me around the dance floor. Blood had dried in the cuts there and bruises colored my pale flesh a deep purple. Arthur kept smiling, his face the same but his teeth sharp and white, a predator's teeth, ready to bite.

People danced in the periphery, or did at first, but soon they vanished into a blur. Only two remained standing, as if keeping watch over me. They were my captors, Gabriel with the golden, tortured eyes, and Syn with the dark, gleaming ones. They watched me, never once taking their gazes from me as we turned and turned. My head hurt and I grew dizzy from it all. I wanted Arthur to stop. I wanted him to let me go, but he wouldn't. He kept hold of me and the more I struggled, the less power it seemed I had. And the less control I had over my body, the wider his grin grew.

It was too fast, the music speeding up, but they all remained as they were. I tried to call out, to tell him to stop, to call to the others, but no one would listen or no one could hear. Then I saw it, saw Arthur take the needle out of his pocket even while he kept twirling me. He brought it to my neck, the gleam in his eyes darkening, turning him into a monster I no longer knew. I screamed then, just before the needle penetrated my skin, just before Gabriel and Syn could reach me, just before I would have to remember the horror of that night.

Sitting upright in the bed, I clapped my hands to my mouth, stifling a scream. Sunlight seeped around the edges of the heavy drapes. I pulled the thick comforter back, noticing I was naked, not surprised by the fact, and covered in sweat. Drawing the curtains back, I peered out the window in time to see a cloud of dust on the long driveway as a Jeep left the property and the gates closed behind it. From my room, I scanned the grounds, noticing the high fence that bordered the vast space.

There was a knock at my door, before it opened. One of the young women who'd served us that first night entered, carrying a tray covered in a white cloth. I held the curtain up in front of me, feeling embarrassed at being seen naked again, but she only smiled and said a hurried good morning before setting the tray down and leaving. That was when I saw the yellow sundress that hung behind the door. On it was pinned a folded note. Taking it off, I opened it and read:

Evangeline,

Syn and I will be gone for part of the day but we will be home in time for dinner. You are free to explore the house but you're not to leave it while we are gone.

Gabriel

I set the note down and took off the lid of the breakfast tray to find a plate of bacon, two eggs, sunny side up, and buttered toast along with a glass of freshly squeezed orange juice and a pretty silver pot filled with coffee. Next to the food was a folded newspaper. I pulled out the chair, poured a cup of coffee and sat down, not sure what I felt exactly when I saw the front page of the paper:

Ransom note received in kidnapping of Evangeline Webb! Wealthy family to pay any price!

I set the coffee down, losing my appetite as I looked at the photographs, one of me taken at a luncheon a month ago, a more recent one of my father looking distraught. I read the article, which said that Arthur had received the ransom note late last night. At the sight of Arthur's name, that weight deep in my belly was back. The amount of money the kidnappers were asking for was atrocious and I flipped to the page where the article continued. That was when I saw why my father looked so distraught. The article said my captors threatened to send me back piece by piece if there was any delay in making the payment.

My stomach turned at the thought, both brothers' faces flashing before my eyes. Could they be so cruel? Had they really, after all they had said last night, sent demands that would threaten such a thing? Had I even been meant to see the paper, or had it been brought in by accident?

There was no clock in the room so I couldn't be sure of the time. I got up and had a quick shower before putting on the sundress. I realized I had no shoes and wondered if they'd done that on purpose so I wouldn't leave the house. Well, it wouldn't matter. I had to get word to my father that I was all right, tell him at least that I was in Mexico somewhere. I had to try to get out of here.

They had said I could roam the house freely, and I would, looking first for a telephone. Their words came back to me, the tenderness both brothers had shown me making me doubt what I'd read. Even when Gabriel had spanked me, it had been more catharsis than punishment. But maybe he hadn't meant it that way at all?

Shaking my head, I went out into the hallway, glancing in either direction toward the two sets of massive doors leading to each brother's suite. My room was situated exactly between them. I wondered which room belonged to which brother, but forced myself to head down the stairs. It didn't matter. They were going to kill me slowly if my father didn't pay the ransom. I needed to get out of here.

"Well, good morning, dear. Or should I say good afternoon?"

I jumped, clutching my chest when I got downstairs to find Caroline dusting the bannister. I'd been so wrapped up in my thoughts that I hadn't seen her.

"Oh! You startled me!"

"I see that," she chuckled.

"Good morning."

"Would you like some coffee?" she asked.

"No thanks. Someone brought breakfast up this morning."

"Oh yes. Well, if you need anything, I'll be in the kitchen. Let me know when you're ready for lunch."

"Ok. I will. Thank you. Um, Caroline?"

She turned, waiting on my question. "When will Gabriel and Syn be back?"

"Oh, it will be early evening I imagine. They told me you're free to explore the house. The library is the most interesting," she said, winking.

"Thank you."

She nodded and walked toward the kitchen, calling to one of the girls. I turned and went down the hall and toward the foyer, glancing behind me as I neared the large front doors. Could I walk out of here? Would no one stop me? It seemed too easy, but I tried the doors anyway.

No, it wouldn't be that easy. The doors were locked.

I continued down toward what appeared to be a large formal living room. It had similar windows to those in the library but no apparent way to open any of them. There was a commotion behind me and I found the front doors opening and Thomas entering, talking to a man I assumed was a gardener by his dirt-caked overalls. They seemed rushed, deep in animated conversation, and didn't see me as they made their way toward the kitchen. Thomas called out to Caroline and I saw why they were in such a hurry — drops of blood dotted the floor where they had walked. The man must have cut himself working. This was my chance.

Moving quickly once they'd disappeared into the kitchen, I slipped out the front door and hurried down the stairs, leaving the path that led to gates that would be closed and disappearing into a thicket of trees instead, determined to climb over the fence at a less obvious point. What I would do once I was out I hadn't yet considered.

※

"Thank you, Caroline," Syn said before hanging up.

"What is it?"

"She's seen the paper. Caroline found it on the tray one of the girls delivered with her breakfast."

"Shit."

"We'll get it cleared up when we're back."

"Is she in the house? Did she actually obey?"

"No, of course not. But I don't think either of us expected her to do as she was told, did we?"

Gabriel smiled and glanced over at his brother. "What would be the fun in that?"

"Thomas will keep an eye on her but I'm not worried she'll get far. She has no shoes and the grounds are secure."

"You ready for this meeting?" Gabriel asked, pulling into the parking lot of a strip mall about two hours from their home.

"I'm ready to put this behind us."

"Think he knew about Eva being on the truck — or was he expecting a dozen girls?" Gabriel asked, killing the engine.

"I have a feeling Eva was a last minute addition."

Gabriel's phone beeped with a new message. He looked at the sender's name. It was their informant. He opened the email:

In case there is any doubt who put her on that truck:

Attached to it was a file that he downloaded and opened. It was the copy of an insurance policy taken out several months earlier. Although the copy wasn't the best quality, it clearly showed that it was a life insurance policy for Evangeline Webb for an absurd amount of money. The beneficiary was Arthur Gallaston.

Then: *The plan was never to sell her. She wouldn't make it that far.*

Attached, was a voice recording but they didn't have a chance to listen to that before the man they were meeting pulled up in a large SUV with heavily tinted windows. Two armed men filed out of it. Syn and Gabriel stepped out of their truck, moved toward the back of the SUV, and climbed in through the open back door. The stale scent of cigar smoke permeated the vehicle and clung to the man inside: Javier Alvarez, the liaison who arranged all the work for the brothers.

In his mid-fifties, Javier Alvarez was a formidable man. They'd first met him shortly after Laney had overdosed, and when she had been pronounced brain-dead, they'd met him again. He had turned up at their door with a proposition for the brothers. Appealing to their grief, and even more so to their rage, he had offered vengeance against the very people whom both Gabriel and Syn held responsible for what happened to their little sister. It was an offer neither could refuse.

"I heard I'm missing a girl," Alvarez said, his voice raspy from years of smoking.

"We're keeping one this time, Alvarez," Syn said. Fuck, the man knew everything.

"Anyone I should know about?" Alvarez asked, something about the way he said it suggesting he already knew.

"No," Gabriel answered, his tone leaving no room for questions.

Alvarez held Gabriel's gaze, but what was inside his eyes was unreadable. Gabriel didn't falter though. He'd decided to keep Eva. That was all there was to it.

Syn held out an envelope. "Thirteen girls worth."

But Alvarez's attention remained on Gabriel.

"Look the other way, Alvarez. We've done it for you plenty of times," Gabriel said. He wasn't one to use threats but neither he nor Syn were above doing whatever they had to do.

"You know Gallaston's fiancée went missing," Alvarez said, taking the envelope.

"Heard about that," Syn replied, keeping his gaze level with Alvarez. "When are you picking up the girls?" he asked, wanting to change the subject.

This was probably one of the most complex and dirty operations the government claimed to know nothing about, but when a shipment like this was intercepted, although Alvarez, Gabriel and Syn all knew the risks involved to the girls, they knew the gamble was worth it. Syn and Gabriel would announce the auction. Remy would arrange for some of the dirtiest men and women in the business to attend, and once they made a purchase, that money was delivered to Alvarez who still managed to turn a profit while collecting enough resources to free the girls and arrest those involved.

Well, arrest the ones they didn't kill, that is.

These were corrupt men and women, drug lords and murderers themselves. Neither Syn nor Gabriel liked to put the women in their paths, but they'd come to accept that sometimes, collateral damage was unavoidable. Normally, Alvarez was able to make his move within a month of the auction — but it was sometimes longer. In the few years they'd been doing this, they'd lost three girls total — and rid the world of twenty-eight of the most unscrupulous criminals in the country. He hoped today's exchange would save twelve more women and return them to their lives while allowing Alvarez and his men to take another dozen scumbags out of circulation. Unfortunately, there was no way of knowing the exact outcome until the next delivery.

"Hope you boys know what you're doing," Alvarez said, nodding to one of his bodyguards sitting in the front seat. The man climbed out, opening the back door to allow Gabriel and Syn to slide out of the SUV. Alvarez opened the envelope and eyeballed the greenbacks, then nodded to the brothers. "Always a pleasure doing business with you."

"Always," Syn said.

Gabriel simply looked on as the back door closed and the SUV drove off.

"I always have to be the social one," Syn said as they climbed back into their truck. "You could at least make some effort."

"I'll leave that to you, brother."

Syn looked out the window as they headed back to the

house to deal with their runaway captive, wondering if he too should feel more remorse over things. Wondering if it were too callous of him to call the lost and potentially lost lives collateral damage. They were innocent human beings, after all.

Gabriel tapped his shoulder, smiling. "I'm not making you think, am I?" he asked, as if having read his mind. "We knew going in what this would be. There's nothing wrong with having come to terms over what we do."

Syn turned to him, burying any pangs of guilt down deep. "Don't worry about me, brother. I'm just anxious to get home. I've got an idea how to deal with our little runaway."

"I have no doubt you do," Gabriel said.

12

My feet were cut and bleeding, my hands scratched and I was no closer to having found a way off the huge property the brothers owned. I regretted not having eaten any of the breakfast now that I felt drained of energy and had to keep reminding myself of what I'd read in the paper, of what they had threatened to do to me in order to get my father to pay.

I could see the top of the house from where I stood near the gates, and part of me wanted to give up, go inside, go up to my room, have a hot bath and lay down. That was when I heard the unmistakable sound of the pickup truck's approach. Adrenaline rushed through me and in a burst of energy, I ran closer to the gates but kept myself hidden as best as I could, crouching down around the three foot wall at the base of the impenetrable fencing, watching now as the tall gates slid open to admit the vehicle. Given the dust the truck rustled up, I was hoping I could hide in it and slip out before the gates closed fully. What I'd do once I was out, I didn't know, but I had to do something.

Staying low, I waited, watching the truck approach, but

when it came to a stop just inside the gates and both doors opened, my heart stopped. Gabriel climbed out of the driver's side and Syn came around from the passenger's side. I remained in my hiding place shielded by bushes to my front and the wall at my right, but something was wrong. Gabriel leaned against the front of the truck with his arms crossed at his chest.

Syn walked right toward me.

"Are you going to make me chase you?" he asked, his steps carrying him closer, his tone delivering a threat as sure as the sun beating down on my back.

I didn't breathe. My heart pounded, a rushing sound in my ears. I rose, my gaze meeting his, and without hesitating — even knowing how fruitless my attempt to escape was — I turned and ran. I ran as if a wild animal chased me, the cuts on my feet opening again with every step, my breath ragged, the crunching of debris with each step loud in my ears. Endurance had never been my sport — I preferred a quiet yoga practice — and Syn was in so much better shape than I was physically. I knew he wasn't close to his full speed, and heard his chuckle behind me even over the sound of the truck moving and the gates closing, sealing me inside. But he let me run, and I knew if he'd wanted to catch me, he would have by now.

I ran. I ran even knowing I had no chance. Every muscle ached, my feet stung and cramps had me clutching my side, but I kept running. I kept going until, finally, inevitably, I tripped over a stone and fell to my hands and knees. I didn't even try to get up. I knew I wasn't going anywhere.

Branches and leaves crunched beneath his steps as Syn closed the space between us, standing before me. My reflection shone in the bright polish of his shoes and slowly, I sat back on my heels and raised my gaze to his.

"You've made me dirty my shoes, Eva," he said, and although he didn't sound angry, his voice quiet and controlled, I knew I would be punished. I knew that this time, *he* would punish me.

I looked down at them, to the bit of dirt that clung to the side of one shoe before peering up at him again, my eyes tearing at what I knew awaited me, what I knew from the gleam in his eye he would take great pleasure in administering.

"I'm sorry."

"Clean them."

I searched his eyes before taking my attention to his shoes. With trembling hands, I reached out to wipe the dirt from them, managing only to smear earth over their otherwise immaculate polish.

Without a word, he closed his fingers over a handful of hair at the back of my head and hauled me to my feet. Whimpering, I rose, covering his hand with my own, trying in vain to alleviate some of the pain. His eyes scanned me from head to toe and with his free hand, he tore the dress from me in one swift motion.

I screamed. It was the only thing I could do as the once pretty yellow material floated down to the ground, leaving me naked and exposed.

"And look at what you've done to yourself with this silly game."

He moved my head so that he forced me to look down at myself, at the cuts on my naked body.

"I don't think you understand, Eva, but perhaps that's our fault," he said, turning me to walk back toward the house, back to where Gabriel stood waiting, his arms folded across his chest, talking to Thomas and Caroline as they all watched our return. I was too far away to hear what Gabriel said to them and Syn's hand tugging painfully on my hair had my full attention.

"Perhaps we've not been very clear about things, although how you misinterpreted this morning's instruction is beyond me."

We reached the driveway and walked on the gravel now, my feet hurting from the little jagged stones.

"You belong to us," Syn continued. "You are now the property of Gabriel and myself."

I looked at him, confused by his words. I knew this, didn't I? I had known it from the moment Syn had said those words to the man who would have bought me: *That one isn't for sale.*

But I *had* been for sale and I'd been bought — by them.

"And we take care of our things," he said, shaking his head as he looked at the state I was in, but at least he released me when we reached the others.

"Just look at what you've done to yourself," Caroline scolded, shaking her head as she looked me over from head to toe.

I looked at Gabriel but he didn't speak, he just watched me, his expression hard, foreboding.

"Let's get her cleaned up," Syn said from behind me. "Caroline, make her something to eat too. I don't want her passing out on me while I'm caning her."

I turned to him, his words chilling me.

"Wouldn't be any fun if that happened, would it?" he asked me.

"I'll serve her dinner early," Caroline said. She pointed to the men. "You'll be eating afterwards?"

Gabriel nodded, his eyes still locked upon me.

"Can you walk or do you want me to carry you?" Syn asked in a deceptively gentle tone.

I looked up at him. He confused me, they both did. They could be so gentle in one breath and in the next, so cruel.

"I can walk," I said.

He gestured for me to go ahead and the three on the stairs leading up to the front doors parted, allowing me to pass. Shame heated my face as I did. I hung my head and walked naked between the brothers as well as the servants, all of them knowing I was about to be punished.

"Up to your room, Evangeline," Gabriel said.

I climbed the stairs with the brothers behind me. Once to my room, Gabriel opened the door for me.

"Into the bathroom."

I obeyed and stood to the side as they ran a bath, checking the temperature before helping me to climb in. My cuts stung, but I lowered myself into the tub as Syn unwrapped a bar of soap and picked up a washcloth.

"Did you send the ransom note?" I asked, tears clouding my vision. "Are you really going to do that to me?" I choked on that part, feeling so completely alone when for some reason, some strange reason, I'd somehow come to trust these two men. The note felt like a betrayal.

Gabriel switched off the water. "You weren't supposed to see the paper," he said, placing his hand on the top of my head. "The girl made a mistake bringing it. Big breath in."

That didn't exactly answer my question, but before I could open my mouth to ask anything else, he pushed on the top of my head, plunging me beneath the water and holding me there. I think I tried to scream as I scrambled to come up for air but his hand prevented me doing so until he pulled me out again.

I gasped for breath, terrified now that they would drown me.

"Once more, this time take that big breath," he said, pushing down again before I could think.

He pulled me back up and took the bottle of shampoo.

"Let me out!" I screamed, wanting out of the tub now, trapped between these two men. "Let me out!"

Water splashed all around the bathroom, leaving large wet splotches on their clothes, but Gabriel's hand on my shoulder stilled me.

"Shampoo, Evangeline. I can't shampoo your hair if it isn't wet."

I looked at him, at the cool front he displayed in words, but knowing the hot anger that lay hidden beneath that exterior. The glimpse I'd had of it at the camp was enough to last a lifetime.

Feeling hopeless, the fight drained out of me. I was powerless and confused as hell. I covered my face, wanting to disappear, wanting to open my eyes and wake up from this nightmare that had become my life. Then the gentlest of fingers began to massage my scalp, the scent of perfumed shampoo soothing, calming me a little.

"Are you really going to do what that note says?" Would they really dismember me piece by piece until my father paid? Was what the newspaper said truly their intention?

"The note wasn't from us, Eva," Syn said. He reached into the tub to take my arm and began to clean it with the sudsy washcloth. "It's not our intention to give you back."

My gaze wandered from Syn's dark eyes to the golden gaze of his brother's. I didn't understand what he had just said. I should have been reassured that they'd not been the ones to send the note, although that raised plenty of other questions, but what he followed with — that they had no intention of giving me back? I couldn't even begin to think about that one.

"Then who? I don't understand."

"We'll discuss it after your bath," Syn said.

"Going under again, Evangeline. Take a breath and relax. I'm not going to let anything happen to you."

Somehow reassured by what could easily have been lies, I took that breath and Gabriel waited for me to do so before pushing me more gently beneath the surface of the water, his fingers combing through my hair, massaging my scalp until the shampoo washed out and he pulled me back up.

"We're pretty sure Arthur's behind that note," Gabriel said while Syn continued with my other arm. "He's now extorting money from your father, or at least he plans to. He must assume you won't be back and now that his plans to have your body turn up have been interrupted, he'll get the cash from a different source."

My body?

"I can't listen to this. I can't."

"Look at these cuts," Syn said, holding up my foot and shaking his head. "Silly girl."

I looked at him with suspicion.

"Stand up, let's finish and we'll get you bandaged."

Gabriel wiped his hands on a towel as I rose to my feet, but when Syn's hand slipped behind me, the washcloth traveling to my most private places, I gasped, grabbing his arm to stop him.

He simply smiled and removed my hand. "I'm going to clean you everywhere, Eva. You'll get used to it. You'll have no secrets from us. You belong to us now."

You belong to us now.

I processed his words slowly, looking off at the white wall while he did as he'd said, his fingers working the washcloth over every inch of my skin. Only when he was satisfied did he have Gabriel wrap a thick towel around me and lift me out of the tub, carrying me into the bedroom and laying me on my bed.

"Let's get these cuts disinfected," Syn said.

I simply lay there, allowing them to work on me, their touch so gentle, so caring. In fact, aside from my parents, I wasn't sure I'd *ever* felt so cared for as I did at that moment. But I had to remember what was coming. I had to remember what Syn had said. He would punish me soon. I watched him as he worked, trying to reconcile those two sides of him, of both of them. Trying to understand their words, their claim that I now belonged to them.

***

Gabriel watched Evangeline closely when they entered the dining room to find Caroline had set a place for her and only for her. Her plate was filled with delicious food, but her comfortable chair had been removed and in its place was a low, hard wooden stool. In the corner of the room stood the foolish girl who had delivered the newspaper to Evangeline's room. The girl's nose was pressed into the corner, the uniform skirt she wore lifted and tucked into the waist to expose her freshly caned bottom. Caroline had done a thorough job of disciplining the girl and he had no doubt Thomas would take the cane to Caroline's own bottom tonight for her oversight.

"Have a seat, Evangeline," Gabriel said when she froze at the sight before them.

She opened her mouth to speak, then closed it again, glancing at the girl in the corner before moving to take her seat. Syn and Gabriel took their places and Gabriel poured a glass of wine for each of them, but left Evangeline's glass empty. She'd drink water tonight. Syn had laid out all he needed for her punishment and he wanted her fully aware for her ordeal.

"You may begin," Gabriel said to her.

She stared at her plate, then looked over at the girl again.

"I'm not very hungry."

"Humor us and eat anyway."

She gave him a sidelong glance but picked up her utensils, lifting the first forkful of salmon to her mouth.

Gabriel and his brother both watched her as she reluctantly ate, forcing down each mouthful she swallowed. He didn't miss the fact that her eyes kept straying to where the punished girl now stood. He'd had Caroline display her there on purpose. He wanted Evangeline to see, to anticipate.

"Did you know Arthur had taken out a life insurance policy on you a few months ago?" Syn asked, taking out his phone and scrolling to the appropriate photo before laying it down on the table and turning it so that Evangeline could see.

"We discussed it. He had one too," she said. "We did that when we bought our house together."

"His was canceled," Syn said, scrolling to the next photo. It had been easy enough to find that bit of information.

She wouldn't look at the image, her pretty eyes darting instead from Syn to Gabriel and back again. Gabriel watched the struggle there, the need to deny, and along with that need, the indisputable knowledge of what was true. She knew it herself. She knew her fiancé was a very bad man. She just hadn't consciously accepted it yet.

Well, that was about to change.

Syn pushed the phone closer to her. "Look at it, Eva."

She shook her head no and instead pushed food around her plate.

"I don't want to."

"What are you afraid of?"

She glanced quickly at Syn, then back at her plate. "Nothing."

"Then look."

With a loud clang, she threw her knife and fork down and took the phone, moving her thumb across the screen. Then she handed it back to Syn who pushed a button to replay the recording he and Gabriel had listened to earlier:

"Sir, moving the timeline up?"

"Just make sure there's only twelve left on that truck at the drop off point. You know what you have to do. No fuck ups, nothing linking back to me. Otherwise, make it look good. And alert me as soon as the others have been dropped."

There was a long silence after that while they watched her process what she'd heard, her eyes brimming with tears at the dispelling of any shadow of doubt.

"What do you want from me?" she finally asked, wiping her eyes.

They remained watching her. Gabriel could see her struggle but would do nothing. Not yet. He needed for her to see. She was the one piece of the puzzle that could put Gallaston away for life. They'd tried before. Alvarez wanted the man's head, but Gallaston was too smart, nothing ever linked him to any of the shipments of either drugs or people. Now, all of that could change. And here before them sat the one person who could make that happen.

"We want you to know that the life you had is over. You won't be going back because if you do, you're dead. We want you to know that it was the man you were months from marrying who did this to you, who put you on that truck like an animal. Who ordered your killing. And we want you to know that this isn't the first shipment of human cargo we've intercepted from Arthur Gallaston, but with your help, it could be the last. You're the missing link, Eva. You're the one who can end this."

She wiped the backs of her hands across her eyes, her defiant gaze locked upon Syn. Gabriel sat back and watched. He would swoop in to comfort her when the time came, but that time wasn't now.

"So you want me to know that my fiancé did this to me. You want me to think that he wanted me dead so he could collect on my life insurance." She choked on that part but managed to compose herself. "That he's the reason you brought me here. He's the reason all those women—" at that she paused, needing a moment before continuing. "That he's the reason that *you* sold all those women at camp to those horrible people." She sucked in a shaky breath, agitation building. They needed to wrap this up. "Fine. I know. But I also know *you're* about to hurt me. *You're* the ones who are about to punish me." Her words were angry as her glance shifted once more to the punished girl in the corner. "What the fuck else do you want? You think I'll be somehow grateful to you? Well, I won't. Not ever!"

Gabriel's fist came down hard on the table, rattling the silverware, making her jump.

"No, Evangeline," he said, pushing his chair back abruptly, loudly. "Your gratitude isn't what we're looking for. We couldn't care less about that. It's your obedience we want. I think you're finished eating."

Syn stood too and tucked his phone into his back pocket.

Evangeline's face crumpled as she looked at them, at

these two men who dwarfed her, who would now give her their undivided attention while they punished her.

"Let's go into the library."

THE LIBRARY. THE ROOM WHERE WE'D BEEN LAST NIGHT, where everything had happened.

I didn't say a word. Arguing didn't make sense. It would only put off the inevitable. I stood, trying to hide the trembling of my hands, my legs, as we walked toward the library. There I saw that they'd been busy preparing for my punishment. In the center of the room was a table and on that table was the cane I recognized along with leather restraints, a thin but sturdy looking chain, a bottle of something and a long hook like thing with a steel ball at the end.

As afraid as I felt about what was coming, there was something else too, some awakening at my core, a tremor in my belly that traveled down to my sex and outward toward my thighs.

I swallowed, awaiting my sentence.

"A dozen strokes and some incentive to stay put when you're told to stay put," Syn said.

Gabriel watched it all silently. Syn was in charge of tonight's punishment.

He picked up the leather restraints first. "Hold out your hands."

I did, knowing there was no alternative. Syn wrapped the cuffs around my wrists and Gabriel picked up the chain, attaching it to the cuffs before running it through a ring attached to a chain hanging from the ceiling above my head. I hadn't noticed that chain the other night. He then pulled on it, drawing my arms up over my head until I stood on tiptoe. He held the other end of it in his hands and waited for Syn to continue.

Syn picked up the bottle and opened it, squeezing some of what I now knew was lubricant onto his fingers, deliberately watching me as he did before coming to stand behind me.

"What's that for?" I asked, shifting a little but unable to go anywhere.

"That incentive I mentioned," he said, one hand gripping my hip and pulling my bottom cheek out.

"Not there, please..."

My plea fell on deaf ears though as his fingers coarsely circled my back hole. I looked up to find Gabriel's golden gaze upon me and my face heated in embarrassment. But that was quickly replaced with a burning pain as Syn pushed his finger inside me.

I cried out, the invasion too fast, but he didn't stop. Instead, he began to move his finger in and out of my bottom, gripping me tightly enough that I remained still as he thoroughly invaded me.

"Please... stop."

At that, the hand that held my hip moved around to clutch my sex. I gasped when his fingers began to work my clit, sending confusing sensations through me, pain opposing the ultimate pleasure of his fingers massaging my wet sex.

I made the mistake of meeting Gabriel's intense gaze as my mouth fell open and Syn added a second finger, lubricating my bottom hole, the sensations coupled with my utter helpless humiliation serving to arouse me like nothing else.

"Your pussy's wet, Eva. Soaked, in fact," Syn said from behind me.

I kept my eyes on Gabriel, my knees weakening beneath me with Syn's continued attentions.

"I'm going to like fucking that dripping pussy later," he whispered into my ear, standing close enough that I felt his cock press against my hip through his pants.

I swallowed, exhaling when he pulled his fingers out, leaving me feeling suddenly empty. I watched as he wiped off his hand, picked up the hook like thing and lubricated the ball at the end. That was when I panicked, when I realized where he intended to put the thing.

"You can't!" I pulled at my restraints but Gabriel held tight and Syn came around behind me once more. "Please... you can't!"

"Shh," Syn said. "Be still now. It's not all bad."

With that, his hand was at my sex again and the pleasure of his fingers battled with fear of what now pressed against my back hole.

"Push against it, Evangeline," Gabriel said. "Like you will when you take my cock inside your ass."

Take him inside... he couldn't do that. Surely...

Gabriel tugged the chain, stretching me a little higher, demanding my full attention.

"Take it in and I'll let you come before I punish you. Be a good girl for us and take it, Eva," Syn said, his fingers working my clit at a frantic pace.

I found myself obeying, pushing against the unyielding steel ball as he slowly worked it inside me, pinching my clit harder, rubbing it faster as he did. Finally, I felt myself stretch at the widest point of it, the sensation of burning, of the thing filling me, the strangest combination of pain and pleasure I'd ever felt, and even through this humiliation, somehow, I came. I came hard, squeezing my legs together around Syn's hand, the walls of my pussy looking for something to close around while my ass took in the ball, the muscles clamping down around the steel as if trying to milk it.

I closed my eyes for an instant or an eternity — I wasn't sure which — but when I opened them again, I found Gabriel's golden gaze on mine, desire having darkened those eyes as he watched his brother make me come.

"Good girl," Syn said when I relaxed my legs and released his hand.

My breathing came hard and fast, my eyes on Gabriel, lust a palpable thing pouring off of him in waves. When Syn gripped a handful of hair and tugged my head back, I opened my mouth to his, wanting him to kiss me, to devour me whole while his brother watched.

I was vaguely aware of Gabriel moving behind me. Syn released me as I heard a click and a moment later, felt pressure on the hook inside my ass. The brothers came around to stand before me and I finally understood what all this meant, why they'd done what they'd done. They had bound me to myself. Standing on tiptoe, the slightest movement would cause the hook to pull, lifting my hips higher the moment I relaxed my feet to stand flat.

Syn picked up the cane then and disappeared behind me. Tears filled my eyes at the pain I knew was moments away, a pain I dreaded but in a way, wanted, needed.

"We'll break this up. Pleasure and pain, Eva. Pain and pleasure. The one always intensifies the other."

With that came the first stroke of the rattan across the lowest part of my ass. I cried out, the pain burning a line of fire across my skin, causing me to stumble forward. But the way the taut chain bound me only allowed me a single step, forcing me to lean forward, the hook keeping my ass lifted and spread to take the next stroke.

"That was pain."

As if I didn't know.

"Count for me"

"One."

The second stroke fell. Gabriel's hands wrapped around my arms to steady me while I groaned, the burning soon becoming an inferno.

"Two. Please..."

Gabriel held me close as the cane struck again. I leaned into him, crying out with the pain, surrendering into Gabriel's strength.

"Say the count, Evangeline," he reminded me before covering my mouth with his for an intense, hot, but all too brief kiss.

"Three." Confusion filled me again as I spoke, my bottom burning, my pussy leaking, the man before me a man I should want to run from, a man whose touch I shouldn't take comfort in.

"Pleasure now," Gabriel said, and the brothers switched places, Syn handing the cane to Gabriel, then slipping in front of me.

Syn kissed me, his hands on either side of my face, my hair matted to cheeks wet with sweat and tears. His tongue entered my mouth and I opened to him, wanting him. One hand moved down, pinching one nipple hard as he went lower, and I heard the zipper of his jeans slide down before feeling the soft head of his cock against my belly. I moaned then, opening wider, pushing myself against him, wanting to rub myself to orgasm.

He leaned slowly down, lifting me slightly, relieving the pressure of the hook in my ass as he brought the head of his cock to my pussy, kissing me now with open eyes, watching me.

"Please," I begged, wanting him inside me, wanting him to fill my pussy as he had filled my ass.

He smiled, slowly sliding into my wet passage. My eyes rolled back with the sensation of his cock inside me, stretching me. The cane stroke that landed then made me gasp against Syn's mouth, pain and pleasure melding as he fucked me slowly.

"Don't forget the count, Eva," he said.

"Four," it was a breathy whisper, but enough because he kept fucking me as Gabriel lay the next stroke down. "Oh..."

I was going to come. I was going to come with Syn in my pussy, a steel ball in my ass and the cane raining fire upon my bottom.

"Five." I moaned, desperate, wanting Syn closer, wanting him to fuck me harder, to make me come.

Gabriel struck again, the sixth stroke at the very tops of my thighs. I cried out, saying the count. Syn pulled out of me and stepped back, leaving me cold and wanting.

I would have reached for him but for my bonds, and as I watched him zip his jeans up, I felt my own arousal dripping down my thighs. I felt the pressure at my back hole lessen as the chain was lengthened and I could stand on flat feet once more. Gabriel set the cane down and I watched, confused as he took the spreader bar that lay on the floor and knelt before me, binding the restraints to my ankles, forcing my legs wide. When he was finished, Syn loosened the chain altogether.

"Kneel," he said.

I obeyed without hesitation, even as I realized the spreader would keep my legs apart as I knelt. He rebound the chain so that my arms were drawn up over my head. It wasn't painful, but it wasn't comfortable either, and because I was so aroused, I was also acutely aware of the steel ball in my ass, of how my sex spread wide, pussy lips gaping. I wanted to come. My bottom burned from the cane, but all I wanted now was to come.

Syn picked up the cane and disappeared behind me again. Gabriel stood before me and opened his pants. My eyes widened at the site of his thick, long cock as he massaged its hard length, the head already wet with pre-cum.

"Open your mouth, Evangeline."

I licked my lips and did, and even as I felt the cane pressed against my ass, the smooth rattan rubbing against the spot he would strike next, I took Gabriel's cock into my mouth, watching him as he closed his eyes and brought one hand to the back of my head.

He groaned, guiding my head over his length. "Suck. Suck harder."

I did, my pussy dripping as I tasted him, wanting him to come in my mouth, wanting to swallow what he gave me. He fucked my mouth slowly, pushing his cock deeper and deeper to my throat. Tears clouded my vision when he went too far too fast, but I wanted to take him deep.

"Pain," Syn said from behind me.

Gabriel pulled his cock out of my mouth. I tugged on my wrists, trying to get hold of him but succeeding only in pulling on the hook.

"That's it, lean forward more. Offer your ass to the cane because when you do, pleasure will come once you've taken the pain."

I did as he said and heard the whipping sound just before a red hot line seared into my trembling flesh. I cried out, pure fire obliterating all thought, my bonds the only thing keeping me from collapsing onto the floor.

"Seven," I called out, remembering.

"Good girl," Gabriel said.

I looked up to find him stroking his cock, the sight filling me with desire again.

"I want..."

He grinned and Syn struck again, drawing another pained cry from me. "Please!"

The chain was adjusted again so that I leaned forward now and my forearms rested on the carpet, my ass lifted at an obscene angle. Gabriel knelt before me, his cock inches from my face.

I heard the cane coming again, the strokes harder now. Syn wasn't holding back.

"Eight!"

Two fingers pushed into my pussy as Gabriel brought his cock to my mouth again. I opened for him, greedy to take all of him.

"You're a dirty girl, Eva," Syn said, fucking my pussy with his fingers. "So, so wet."

They retreated at once and Syn struck the hardest stroke yet. I screamed with it and he didn't wait for me to count now. Instead, he delivered the final three in quick succession, no pleasure between the strokes, only pain now.

I wept from it, from the all-encompassing hurt, wanting the pleasure but feeling only the pain. I heard the cane tossed aside and realized Syn was breathing harder behind me.

"Shh," Gabriel said, coming closer again. "It's over."

I opened my mouth when he pressed his cock against my lips, and as I did, I felt the tugging on my back hole along with Syn's instruction to push. I did, sucking Gabriel's cock all along, and when the hook was out of my ass, I felt Syn settle between my knees, felt the head of his cock at my pussy, his fingers coming to my clit. I moaned around

Gabriel's cock when Syn entered me and even as Gabriel gripped my head and fucked my mouth hard, Syn did the same to my pussy, his fingers rough on my clit.

I came first, the burning heat of my punishment intensifying the pure pleasure of being taken like this, of having them both, one in my mouth, the other in my cunt, being fucked like a whore. Soon Gabriel's cock swelled in my mouth and the rhythm of Syn's fucking quickened, and the two men exploded inside me, their groans sending me over the precipice again. I was only pleasure now, moaning my climax around the thick cock in my mouth, swallowing Gabriel's salty essence, taking Syn's seed deep inside me. When it was done and Gabriel pulled his cock from my lips, I brought my fingers to my mouth, capturing what spilled from my lips. Then Syn slid out from deep inside me, the residue of his seed wet on my thighs. I closed my eyes, collapsing, the carpet rough beneath me. Pressing my legs together, I rubbed my still tender clit, quiet while they watched me as a small tremor shook me one final time.

13

It was the middle of the afternoon when I woke. I turned over onto my back only to flop back onto my belly with a pained groan, my bottom tender from last night's punishment. I lay my cheek back down on the pillow to think.

Arthur. The evidence against him was damning. I hadn't wanted it to be true, I hadn't wanted Arthur to be the bad guy, but when I'd heard the recording, heard his voice, I knew he was. Although the memories hadn't yet returned, I could no longer deny who had put me on that truck.

The voice on the recording I'd recognized as Jamison's, but what had Arthur's instruction truly meant? I couldn't believe what Gabriel and Syn were suggesting — that Arthur never meant for me to make it off that truck. That he wanted me dead? No, it couldn't be. Murder? He couldn't do that... could he? Was that why he'd taken out that life insurance policy? Did he hate me so much that he'd kill me even though, once he'd married me, he'd have had access to my family's fortune anyway?

I turned back over and sat up, flinching with the pain

but wanting it, too. My head hurt from this line of thinking and I needed a distraction. Gabriel and Syn came to mind, their faces stern, yet also something else. They were cruel, they would be obeyed without question — but there was more. Was I stupid to think they weren't just toying with me? There was more to these men than that. They'd punished me while making me come, the orgasms like nothing I'd ever experienced before. The taste of Gabriel's cock in my mouth only made me want more of him. Feeling Syn slide his thick length into my pussy while I sucked his brother's cock — the thought and the images it conjured up had me wet even now. I felt desirable, wanton, lustful. It was completely new. I'd never felt anything even close to this with Arthur. Sex with Arthur had been... ordinary. Orgasms with him were different, and now that I'd felt what a real orgasm was, what I'd experienced before would never again be enough.

I shook my head and turned back over onto my side. My captors had fucked me and I had wanted them. I hadn't resisted, not even a little. I could blame the bonds all I wanted to, but I knew the truth. And now I was making a romance out of it.

God, what was wrong with me? What was I thinking? They may have saved me from one evil but weren't they only a different sort of evil? They could keep me locked up here forever. They could kill me tomorrow. The story about their sister, could that have been true? They could tell me anything they wanted to.

But I'd never forget the look in Gabriel's eyes when he'd played that recording. No man could feign that level of pain, could he?

I thought back to the previous night, to Syn's words. What had they meant that I was the missing link? The thing that could end this? Did they expect me to believe they were the good guys?

I pushed the blankets away and stood up. I couldn't think about this, not anymore. I went into the bathroom and started the shower, catching a glimpse of myself in the mirror. My hair was a tangled mess, probably a combination of sleep and sex, and my eyes were puffy and red.

I looked away, opening a few drawers until I found a toothbrush which was still in its packaging, along with some toothpaste. Smearing the stuff onto it, I brushed my teeth, then climbed into the shower and stood under the hot water, trying to clear my mind, to think only of the droplets of water drumming against my skin, knowing this wasn't some dream I was going to wake from.

I stood there for as long as I could until the water started to cool, the humidity of the room making me feel weak. Switching the water off, I climbed out, wrapped myself in a thick towel and walked back out into the bedroom only to stop short when I found Gabriel standing at one of the windows, drinking a cup of coffee as he gazed out into the garden.

"You slept late," he said, looking me over. "How do you feel?"

Unable to answer, I hugged the towel tighter to myself. I felt afraid of him, more so now that I was alone with him. What he'd done to me at the camp, that whipping, Syn making him stop... it frightened me still.

Gabriel exhaled and looked away, rubbing the back of his neck. It was a moment before he turned back to me. "What happened at camp, what I did to you... I was wrong."

I listened, seeing how difficult this was for him, shocked he was saying anything at all.

"I was angry — not at you, not really, but I was angry and I shouldn't have punished you angry."

I couldn't speak. He was apologizing? To me? Everything about him now said he was genuine. But when he took a step forward, I took one back.

Gabriel stopped, holding up his hands. "I don't want you to be afraid of me. It won't happen again, not in anger. I promise."

I studied him, seeing him in the sunlight. I didn't understand this man. There was something about him that compelled me to trust him, to believe him, to hide myself in his embrace and take shelter there. His words now only reinforced those feelings. I needed to steel myself though, to look at the facts, at actions — not at stupid feelings. Hadn't the past few days shown me what a great judge of character I was?

"Thank you for saying that," I managed. "I can see it was difficult for you to do."

Clearly, it wasn't the response he was hoping for, but he nodded, covering his mouth for a moment, emotions swirling in his eyes, emotions which he closed off from me in an instant.

"How do you feel?" he asked.

"How do I feel?" Did he expect me to say that I was okay? I was a freaking mess. "I feel confused. I feel angry, I feel... stupid." I sat down on the bed, flinching when my bottom made contact. "I don't know... I don't understand."

He listened but didn't question me. "I brought you some coffee. If you're hungry, Caroline can make you a sandwich."

I was far from hungry. "What's going to happen to me?"

"We won't hurt you if that's what you're worried about."

"You hurt me last night."

"I didn't say we wouldn't punish you when you deserved it. And as far as last night goes, you came two, three times?"

I glanced away, feeling my face flush hot. I picked up the coffee mug on the nightstand and took a long sip before turning back to him. "Then what do you want with me?"

Gabriel took a step toward me and set his mug down. "Same as last night, I'd like your obedience. Lay down on your belly so I can have a look at any bruising," he said, stacking the pillows beside me at the edge of the bed.

"I'm fine," I said, gripping my mug more tightly.

"You're far from fine. Now do as you're told."

"No." My heart was racing and it seemed as though my mouth worked without my brain's permission.

A soft smile spread across Gabriel's face.

GABRIEL EXHALED, PUSHED ASIDE THE PILLOWS HE'D JUST stacked and sat down beside her. He could see the little pulse at her neck moving fast and her knuckles had gone white around the coffee mug.

"We got off on the wrong foot, but I've apologized now. Whether or not you can accept that apology is your choice, but it doesn't change anything between us. You are under my command — mine and my brother's. You will do as you're told or you will face consequences. Now you know we don't mind getting rough, but I'd like for you to see a gentler side. Pleasure and pain, Evangeline. We give both…generously."

She swallowed, her eyes going a little wider.

"Now, I can make you do as I say," he began, prying her fingers from the coffee mug and setting it down on the nightstand. "But I'd really like for you to simply do as you're told. It will be easier for both of us."

The girl was trembling, paralyzed it seemed. He cupped his hands around hers and offered her a small smile. "I have some ointment which will make you feel better," he said. "Do as I say and you'll be allowed to write your father a letter."

"I will?" She looked so hopeful, so innocent — that innocence reminding him of his sister. Once she'd been innocent and naïve too.

He nodded. "I keep my word, always Evangeline. You can count on that."

She considered, studying him. "I'm embarrassed," she said, a flush confirming her words.

Gabriel smiled at her sweet honesty.

"No need. I'm here to take care of you."

Her eyes searched his and finally, she lowered her lashes and nodded. "Okay."

He stood back, his cock already beginning to harden in anticipation at the deep red blush coloring her throat and face. Without looking at him, she stood, unwrapping the towel from around herself before shyly turning to lay over the stack of pillows.

Gabriel took in the sight of her as she waited there, bent over the bed, her pretty little bottom displayed for him. He stepped closer, inspecting her skin, the bright sun across her pale flesh illuminating the row of pink stripes, a neat dozen of them lining her bottom and upper thighs, along with a few lingering bruises from the strap. She kept her legs tightly together, clenching her cheeks.

"Relax your muscles for me, Evangeline," he said, waiting. "When you're told to bend over for us, you're to keep everything soft and you're never to close your legs like that. You belong to us, remember."

She made a sound of protest but slowly separated her legs, relaxing her muscles until the round buttocks unclenched. His cock stood at attention now as he glimpsed the offering between her thighs. He'd get more than a glimpse in a minute though.

Adjusting his cock, he opened the nightstand drawer where he'd earlier placed what he needed. He first took the jar of ointment and opened it, sitting on the edge of the bed next to her.

"When I say you belong to us, it means your pretty little pussy belongs to us as well," he said, softly smearing the stuff onto her bottom, gently massaging as he did.

She didn't speak, keeping her face buried in the blankets instead. That was fine. In no time, he'd be hearing those sweet little sounds she made when she came.

Her skin was smooth, the round buttocks soft against his palms as he massaged her flesh, pressing a little harder as she relaxed to his touch, his fingers moving closer to the split between her cheeks while she lay unmoving and obedient.

"Open your legs a little wider for me," he said, his hands coming to her thighs, rubbing more of the ointment into the tender flesh, his thumb grazing her swelling clit as her legs eased apart, causing her to gasp.

"That's it, just relax," he said, touching her clit, rubbing the tender nub between his fingertips. Her hips writhed in response, her head coming off the bed, her hands fisting in the blankets.

Gabriel smiled, placing a finger at the very top of the cleft of her bottom. "And your little bottom too belongs to us," he said, waiting for her to understand. "I want to see that pretty bottom hole now, Evangeline," he said, sliding his finger down the crevice while he continued to massage her clit.

But she tensed at his words, her entire body going rigid.

"Please," she begged, her voice muffled as she buried her face in the blankets.

"Shh, relax and stay soft. There's nothing to be embarrassed about. I have a right to look at what belongs to me, and right now I want to see that pretty little bottom hole," he said, his fingers working slowly, rubbing circles over her swollen clit. "Let me take care of you now. Let me give you pleasure like you did me last night."

The tentative glance over her shoulder showed him how her eyes had darkened, the pupils having dilated. She turned to face forward again, but her body relaxed and he resumed his attention to her clit while with his other hand, he spread her cheeks to expose her back hole.

"This sexy little hole is mine," he said, touching it. "Has anyone fucked your ass, Evangeline?" he asked, still massaging, anticipating her tensing.

She made some desperate whimper and Gabriel smiled.

"Tell me, have you ever been fucked in the ass?" he probed, enjoying her discomfort.

She covered her face with her hands and pressed it into the blankets while shaking her head.

"That pleases me more than you can imagine, Evangeline. I'm happy to know I'll be the first to fuck your tight little asshole."

She moaned as he worked her clit faster while circling the ointment over her back hole.

"You like that, don't you? You like me playing with your pussy, your bottom?"

She groaned and he was sure she wasn't breathing given how she'd pushed her face into the blankets.

"Tell me, Evangeline, do you want me to stop or should I continue?"

When she didn't answer, he pulled away. That made her lift her head and look back at him.

"Tell me," he said again.

"Don't stop. Please."

He smiled. "Reach back and spread your bottom cheeks open for me," he said, taking the tube of lubricant out of the drawer and opening it. "I need you to hold yourself open while I do this next part or I'll have to stop playing with your clit to do it myself."

She swallowed but slowly reached back to pull her bottom cheeks apart.

"Wider," he said. "And you may watch."

To encourage her, he brought his hand back to her clit. She pulled her bottom cheeks wider, exposing herself fully to him, looking back to watch as he poured a generous amount of lubricant onto her bottom hole.

"That's it. You're doing very well." He put the lube down, bringing his fingers to her back hole to smear the stuff in.

"Oh..." She lifted her hips higher and lay her face back down, closing her eyes. "I'm going to come," she barely managed when he slid one finger deep into her ass. "Oh... I..."

She arched her back high, squeezing her thighs together as the muscles of her back hole clamped down around his finger, pulsing around it as she came quietly, her toes curling, her hands moving to pull handfuls of the blankets into her chest, her eyes squeezed tight, her mouth open in a small O. Gabriel added a second finger to her asshole, fucking her slowly, not letting up when she opened her eyes again, gasping, widening her stance while trying to pull away from him.

"No, Evangeline. I'm not finished with your bottom yet. Stay right where you are," he said, pulling his fingers out of her ass and rising to his feet. She watched as he unzipped his jeans to release his engorged cock, massaging its length as she watched.

"I can't fuck your ass without preparing you," he said. "Your pretty little asshole is too tight to take this just yet, isn't it?" he asked, showing her his length

Her eyes went wide, her mouth opening a little before she returned her gaze to his and nodded.

Gabriel smiled. "No, I need to stretch you to take me first."

She made a quiet sound, swallowing.

"Slide you hand between your legs," he instructed.

She squeezed her eyes shut and buried her face in the blankets.

Gabriel chuckled and caressed her hip. "Look at me, Evangeline. I watched you squeeze your thighs together and come last night. Syn and I both did. Now I want to watch you while you play with yourself."

"No," came the sound muffled by the blankets.

"Yes." He scratched his fingernails down her back from her shoulder to her hip. It wasn't hard, but it made her look at him. "Put your hand between your legs and rub your clit. It will help you relax, help your bottom open to take the plug."

She shook her head again.

"Remember what I said earlier and do it *now*, Evangeline."

At the sternness of the *now*, she looked away but slid her

hand down between her legs and tentatively began to rub her pussy while Gabriel watched.

"Good girl," he said, rubbing his length. "Have you ever watched a man masturbate?"

"No."

He tucked his cock back into his pants to her obvious disappointment. "Then let's get you plugged and you can watch me while I watch you finger your little pussy, what do you think?"

She nodded, arching back again, two fingers pressing hard against her clit as she bit her lip and squeezed her eyes shut.

"Let's get that ass filled. Don't come yet. Just watch."

She did, looking at him over her shoulder, her eyes widening as he smeared lubricant over a mid-sized butt plug. It would be uncomfortable for her to wear, but it would make taking him in her ass easier that night.

"Push against it," he said, coming down on one knee behind her, spreading her open with one hand and placing the head of the plug at her entrance. "Play with yourself while you do and push. Imagine it's me pushing my cock into your tight little asshole."

She was so good. "Good girl, that's it." Gabriel watched her close her eyes, her fingers working over her clit, her asshole relaxing, opening, stretching as he patiently pushed it into her and pulled it back out, fucking her ass with the plug, moving slowly, even though his own cock was ready to explode.

While he worked the plug, he kissed then bit her plump buttock, and she gasped. He did it again and this time she moaned, her body tensing when the widest part of the plug stretched her tiny hole. He held there, adding a little more pressure but not wanting to force it in until her body relaxed and the plug sank in to its neck and her muscles closed around it.

"Good girl," he said, standing. "Come here, on your knees before me."

She slid to the floor and he could see from her face that the plug was uncomfortable. Well, she'd get used to it. He pushed his jeans down and brought the tip of his cock to her mouth.

"Lick it for me," he said. "Lick my cock but don't stop playing with your pussy."

She opened her mouth and closed her eyes, licking, tasting, closing her lips around him, making him moan while he pumped his cock.

"That's it, now open your eyes and watch. It's what you want to see, isn't it?"

She sat back a little, careful, he noticed, to keep her bottom on her heels.

"Spread your knees wider so I can see that pussy," he said, pumping faster. "And thrust your tits out to me. I'm going to come on them."

Gabriel pumped harder, tension building in his cock, as her fingers worked faster. She kept her glittering gaze on him though, only closing her eyes when she threw her head back, crying out, her orgasm finally taking her.

Watching her come pushed him over the edge and he fisted a handful of hair with one hand. Her eyes flew open just as the first spurt of pearly semen struck her breasts and he watched her watch him come, wide eyed, Gabriel groaning, pumping ropes of the thick seed across her chest.

GABRIEL'S ARMS WRAPPED AROUND ME, LIFTING ME TO THE

bed. I was very aware of the plug and shifted to my side while he went into the bathroom and returned with a warm washcloth to clean me thoroughly.

"You okay?" he asked. He could be so gentle, yet so harsh. It was the strangest thing.

I nodded. "This doesn't feel good." I pointed to my bottom, feeling heat at my neck and face as I did, although I wasn't sure why that was. It wasn't as though he hadn't inspected, touched, punished or tasted every inch of me.

That thought only embarrassed me even more.

"You'll get used to it and you'll be grateful to have had it later. Here," he said, opening a drawer in the dresser and taking out a pink dress. "Put this on."

Grateful for any clothing, I unzipped it and slipped it over my head. When I reached back to zip the dress, Gabriel came up behind me and did it himself, holding me where I stood before him, his gaze meeting mine in the mirror. He stood more than a head taller than me, his hands on my waist. If anyone were to see us now, we'd look like a normal couple.

"You said I could write a letter?"

He nodded. "Yes, and you need to eat something. You don't eat enough, Evangeline."

Once we got downstairs, Gabriel walked me into the kitchen where Caroline and two girls were busy preparing the next meal.

"Caroline, how about a sandwich for Evangeline?"

The woman looked at me and smiled.

"Sure, Gabriel. Anything special you'd like, dear?"

She was so odd, Caroline. She looked like a sweet, plump aunt, but I'd seen what she had done to the girl's bottom the other night. In fact, I saw that same girl chopping vegetables at the counter and knew exactly how her bottom looked underneath that uniform skirt. Yet here was Caroline, sweet as can be. I didn't understand.

"Anything is okay." I didn't care what I ate.

"We'll be in the library," Gabriel said, leading the way. We found Syn sitting behind his desk, laptop open, the sound of fingers on the keyboard. He looked up as soon as we walked in.

"Good morning," he said, his gaze sliding over my body, taking in every detail. "Or..." He checked his watch and stood. "Good afternoon. You look very pretty, Eva."

A few moments later, Caroline entered. Neither brother seemed startled or surprised at the way she had come into the room without so much as a knock. I worried that someday, she'd walk in that same way when I was being punished — or worse.

The tray she carried held a single plate with my sandwich, along with a tall glass of water "Where shall I set it?" she asked.

"Here on my desk is fine," Gabriel said. "Thank you."

Caroline set the tray down and quietly left. I eyed the sandwich and my stomach growled.

Gabriel didn't miss it and smiled tenderly. "Here," he said, picking up the plate and water. "Why don't you kneel here? I don't imagine you want to sit down."

Gabriel set the plate on top of one of the ottomans. I knelt down to eat but Syn stopped me.

"Just a moment, Eva," he said, pushing the ottoman back. "When you're asked to kneel, I'd like you to keep your knees wide and sit back on your heels. Your pretty little pussy should always be available to us."

I swallowed, hearing my own breathing come a little faster as I obeyed, opening my legs to them, looking down to find the lips of my pussy gaping. Strangely, I didn't *want* to close my legs, didn't want to hide myself.

"Good girl," Syn said, pushing the ottoman toward me.

I picked up my sandwich and ate while the brothers spoke together in Spanish. I could follow bits of the conversation but they spoke in hushed tones that made it difficult for me to hear and understand it all. It sounded like Syn had an e-mail he wanted to show Gabriel. I watched from my place, nibbling on my sandwich, a delicious goat cheese with roasted peppers and eggplant tucked into a French baguette.

"When did you get it?" Gabriel asked, standing next to his brother and looking at whatever was on Syn's monitor.

"Just an hour ago. It's not the best quality image but I imagine there will be more frames. I'll collect them all before the end of the day. I don't think there can be any doubt after this."

"I agree," Gabriel said, casting a quick, concerned glance my way.

I remained silent chewing a small bite of my sandwich, wondering what they were talking about, part of me not wanting to know.

I set my sandwich down. "You said I could write a letter to my dad," I reminded Gabriel.

"Finish your sandwich first."

I nodded and ate quickly, then drank the glass of water. "May I have a cup of tea?" The fact that I asked seemed to please them.

Gabriel picked up the phone and pushed a button that I assumed connected him to the kitchen because he asked for a pot of tea to be brought in. While we waited for it, he remained silent, we all did, and I wondered if he had changed his mind.

"You promised," I said.

He put up a hand telling me to wait when the door opened and one of the girls brought in a pot of tea and single cup. The girl cleared away the empty plate and glass, and Syn thanked her. Then she was gone as swiftly as she'd come.

Syn poured a cup of tea and brought it to me. "Do you take milk or sugar?"

I shook my head and took the cup he held out for me. "You promised I could write a letter."

"And I told you I always keep my promises," Gabriel said, his tone curt. He reached into his pocket and retrieved his cell phone.

"But would you prefer to call and talk to him?"

I looked up, my heart pounding suddenly. "What?"

He held the phone and waited for me to reply.

"You'd... let me?"

They'd be taking a huge chance handing me a phone. For one thing, the call could be traced. I could blurt out information even knowing I'd be punished. Although it wasn't as if I knew my location.

"I would, on two conditions."

"What conditions?"

"You won't have long, I won't take a chance on the call being traced."

I nodded, still waiting, still not truly believing he would let me do this. Even a moment to hear my father's voice, for him to hear mine, was invaluable.

"You're only to tell him that you're safe and not to pay the ransom, but nothing else."

It would be easier for me to hate them if they were cruel to me.

I nodded. "Okay. What's the second condition?"

"Your submission."

I was confused. Didn't they have that already? Not when they bound me, I understood that, but so far, I had done what I'd been told to do, hadn't I? I had submitted to them, but I'd done it out of fear. They had taken it from me, even in those moments where they'd given me pleasure. It would be easier to justify being made to because to be forced to submit was easier to accept than giving myself freely to men I should hate.

Either way, whether I submitted or not, they would have me. They could do whatever they wanted to do to me, we all knew it, but they were asking for my submission.

If I wrote a letter, there was no way to say for sure that they would mail it. I knew we were in Mexico somewhere and their house was far from any town. It would take effort to mail it, and they'd likely send it from a location far enough away to make it impossible to link it back to the house. Wherever that was. If I could talk to my dad though, if I could hear his voice, if he could hear mine, it would set his mind at ease, if only a little.

"You'll have my submission."

Gabriel nodded.

"What's the number?"

I told it to him. It was a direct line to my father, one reserved just for family.

Gabriel punched in the numbers then looked at me before completing the call. "Take care that you only tell him what we've said. If you try to give away any information..."

"I won't." They were putting their trust in me — and I wanted to show them they could. I held out my hand. "I promise."

He nodded and pushed the final button to make the call and a few moments later, handed me the phone.

"Hello? This is Victor Webb," my dad said.

"Dad?"

It broke my heart to hear the choked sound on the other end of the phone line.

"It's me, dad. It's Evangeline."

"Evangeline! Oh, God... are you all right? Honey, are you hurt?"

Tears fell as I shook my head. "No. I'm not hurt." But I wasn't okay either. "Dad?" He sounded like he was crying.

"Where are you honey? Does someone have you?"

I looked up at the brothers. They watched me intently but, thankfully, I saw neither malice nor anger in their eyes.

"Yes, but" — Gabriel made a motion with his finger to move it along — "that note you got, it's a lie. I never went jogging, dad. Don't pay it. Whoever is sending that note doesn't have me."

"Honey? Are you sure? Where are you? Tell them I'll pay whatever they want." Another choked sound. "Anything."

Gabriel gestured for me to wrap it up. I shook my head, but he raised his eyebrows and I reluctantly nodded.

"I have to go, dad," I barely managed. "I'll try to be in touch again soon though. As soon as I can. Just don't pay it, okay? And if there's anything else sent," I said, choking on the words myself. "Don't believe it. I'm not being hurt."

"Where are you, baby?"

"I don't... I can't say. I have to go now, dad." Gabriel reached for the phone but I held on to it and turned away so he wouldn't take it. "I love you."

"I love you."

Those were the last words I heard before Gabriel took the phone from my hands and ended the call.

Syn stood looking down at me while I remained on my knees wiping tears with the backs of my hands. When I turned my face up, he held his hand out to me. I studied him for a long moment, but slowly took the offered hand, letting him help me to my feet while Gabriel slipped the phone into one of the desk drawers.

"Thank you for letting me do that," I said, feeling anxious.

"You're welcome."

"Will you let me call him again? Was that true, what you said?"

"I told you already that I won't lie to you," Gabriel answered.

I thought about that, about all of the lies in my life. My whole engagement was a lie.

I slipped my hand out of Syn's and took a step back, looking at each brother in turn, wondering if they knew what I was thinking now, if it was obvious: the second condition.

"Undress, Evangeline," Gabriel said.

I kept my gaze upon him as I quietly pulled the dress over my head and set it on the nearby ottoman.

"Turn around and show Syn how I've decorated your bottom."

As much as I dreaded this, knowing the impossibility of escaping this embarrassment, I couldn't deny the sudden heat between my legs at Gabriel's command.

Meeting Syn's gaze for a moment, I struggled to fully accept the strange, conflicting emotions I felt. I turned my back to him and waited, my heart racing, every hair standing on end, my pussy already slick. What had happened to me? Not an hour ago, I had come watching Gabriel masturbate over me. I could still remember the warm streams of semen across my breasts, and yet here I was, wanting. Again.

The room was absolutely still for a moment before I felt Syn's hand at my shoulder, leaning me forward a little as the fingers of his other hand grazed the marks on my bottom, then touched the jeweled end of the plug protruding from between my cheeks. Even that smallest of touches made me gasp.

And Syn didn't miss it. Although he didn't say a word, his light touch against my pussy told me he knew.

"So pretty. I think we should always keep her marked."

"I agree," Gabriel said.

I could now tell whose fingers were whose as they traced the lines of last night's punishment.

"You chose a rather large plug," Syn said, his hand flattening against my low back, the touch gentle but demanding, pushing me forward.

"I did, but if she's going to take my cock in her tight little ass, she needs it stretched wide."

"An anal virgin. You're a lucky man, brother."

The fact that they talked about me as if I weren't there shamed me, but it was that very shame that heated my sex through.

"The hair grows back so roughly after it's shaved though, doesn't it?" Gabriel asked.

Syn agreed. "I was noticing that. Clara's due in about a half hour. We'll have her waxed this time."

Clara again? Waxing?

I must have made a sound because Syn patted my bottom twice. "Shh, it's all right. Waxing only hurts for a second or two. Or so I'm told. And I think we both like the look and feel of your bare, soft pussy, don't we, Gabriel?"

I looked over my shoulder to see Gabriel nod his head. "Why don't you go on up to your room, Evangeline? I'll send Clara up as soon as she's here," he said, helping me to rise and turning me to face him, his hands gentle on my bare arms. "I'm proud of you," he said, a small smile curving his lips. "I think we're learning to trust each other."

"Do I have to be waxed? I can shave myself."

Both Gabriel and Syn laughed aloud at that and Gabriel turned me to give my bottom a pat. "I prefer you waxed so yes, you do. Go on upstairs and wait for Clara now."

"Ugh." I picked up the dress and slipped it over my head, twisting my hands behind me to zip it, but not looking back at them. I felt their gazes upon me as I left, heard their quiet satisfied chuckles as I closed the door behind me.

14

I had barely been in my bedroom for thirty minutes when there was a knock on my door and Syn opened it, allowing Clara to enter. I stood and smoothed the dress down over my legs, nervous.

Clara set her things down and closed the door. She then began to roll up her sleeves while Syn spoke to her in Spanish. She looked at me and nodded.

Syn turned to me. "I'm going to take the plug out for Clara to do her work, Eva. Bend over the foot of the bed for me."

"Syn, please. Can't I do this myself?"

He had walked over to me by then and pulled me in for a quick hug, a gesture of unexpected affection. "It'll be fine. Now come on, it will only take a few minutes once we get the plug out. I'll be here with you and when it's done, I'll get you plugged again and you can relax for the afternoon. Remember what you promised us before you called your father."

"Fine." If it would help me to get another call to my dad,

or more, then I'd do it. I'd submit. I wondered how much more they would expect of me.

"Bend over the bed and lift your dress."

I was still moist from the episode over Gabriel's desk and Syn's words added to that lingering arousal. I glanced once at Clara who watched silently, then bent over the bed and lifted the skirt of my dress.

"Good girl," Syn said, pulling one cheek out to twist the plug a few times. He instructed me to push as he finally took it out altogether. "There."

My face burned hot as I realized he was looking at my bottom hole, at my *stretched* bottom hole.

"Looks good. We'll slip it back in once Clara's finished." At that, he nodded, and the waiting woman approached. Since I was already bent over, she did the back first. The strips of wax hurt as she yanked each one off, but she worked quickly, and it was over much sooner than I'd feared. She then told me to turn over in Spanish. Syn began to translate for me but I stopped him.

"I understand Spanish," I said, locking my gaze with his, letting him know I had at least heard and understood some of his conversations with Gabriel.

He raised an eyebrow. "Get into position then."

I lay on my back, opening my legs and Clara began. The closer she got to the seam of my sex, the more painful it became. But I grit my teeth, and mercifully, it was over within fifteen minutes. Clara stood, cleaned up her things and turned to go. Syn leaned over me, his keen gaze scanning my now naked mound. Then he grabbed one of the pillows, set it down on the edge of the bed and told me to bend over it.

"Wait for me like that, your skirt raised. I'll see Clara out before I plug you."

"Yes, sir."

He smiled at that and I assumed the position, my pussy growing more and more aroused while I waited. I looked over at the plug. He'd left it on the nightstand along with the lubricant. It was a large plug but Gabriel's cock was bigger. The thought of him taking me in my bottom scared me even as it excited me.

I shook my head. Something was wrong with me. I was aroused by the thought of being fucked by my kidnappers?

But I didn't see them as my kidnappers, not really. Not anymore.

My mind shifted to that night again, the night I'd followed Arthur.

"Ready?" Syn asked.

"Yes," I said, both startled and relieved at the interruption of my thoughts.

"I like you like this, Eva," he said.

I looked over my shoulder to find his eyes on my ass. I felt embarrassed but in a way, I liked it too. I liked him looking at me like this.

"I like looking at your ass. I like you lying there and allowing it," he shifted his gaze to mine, "enjoying it perhaps?"

I couldn't deny the arousal I felt. My lying here like this, it was what they wanted. They had asked for my submission, and giving it excited me. Even so, speaking those thoughts out loud would be impossible.

"Take your dress off, turn over and open your legs wide. Show me your pussy."

I did as he said, sitting up to take off the dress before opening my legs, baring myself to his gaze.

"Pull your knees up and keep them spread."

I did, unable to take my gaze from his while he stood

over me, watching. Once I was in position, Syn stepped closer, pushed my knees even wider then pulled my pussy lips apart, just looking at my sex before inhaling deeply.

"I like how you smell when you're wet."

Without ever breaking eye contact, he lowered his face and opened his mouth to run his tongue over the length of me. I sucked in a breath as he circled my clit with the tip of it before licking again, his hands on my thighs, holding me wide. I watched the top of his head then as he buried his face in my pussy, his mouth soft and hot and wet, licking and sucking, making me gasp, making me hug me knees in closer, making me grind myself against his face until I almost fell apart. But just as I was about to come, he stopped and looked at me again, his lips shiny and swollen, the pupils of his eyes dilated.

"I love how you taste, but right now, I need to fuck you," he said, straightening, unzipping his jeans.

My attention went immediately to his hard, ready cock, the tip of it glistening with pre-cum, making me lick my lips. When he laid his weight on me, I reached for him, wanting him. I felt his cock at the entrance of my pussy and smelled my smell on his lips when he brought his mouth to mine, teasing me with the briefest of kisses, his cock sliding slowly into my passage.

"I love your cunt," he said, kissing again, our mouths open, as he licked, then bit my lip. "I love your tight little cunt hugging my cock."

I gasped because he thrust into me then, watching me when he did, drawing my wrists up over my head, kissing me again, our eyes locked as he drew out slowly and thrust again.

"You like me fucking your cunt, don't you?" he asked.

My breath came in gasps between his kisses and neither

of us closed our eyes for more than a blink. I tried to speak, but all I managed was some strange sound set off by his now harder thrusting.

"Tell me," he said, still kissing me, the thrusts deeper, harder, faster, "tell me. Do you like my cock inside your wet little pussy, Eva?"

I nodded, it was all I could manage as I pushed my hips up to meet his thrusts, my clit rubbing against him, his movements coming faster now, his cock swelling inside me, signaling his imminent release.

"Tell me," he said once more, his voice rougher, his grip on my wrists harder.

"Yes... I like... oh... Syn... I'm going to come."

His fierce gaze locked on mine when I said it, as if he were intent on watching me come. It wasn't the earth shattering orgasms I'd had with them before, and it wasn't one that tore me apart either. This one came on slow, swelling at my core, wound tight as he pumped into me repeatedly, the only sounds that of our breathing, the wet noise of our fucking. When I felt him shudder and throb inside me, that tight ball gave way and I sucked in a breath and would have closed my eyes but for his command to keep them open, to keep them on him.

He didn't speak after that, his breathing shorter, his thrusts faster, harder, his black eyes taking on a shine until he stilled inside me, his mouth on my cheek, his eyes glued to mine. I came. I came with him, my eyes open, wanting to see, wanting him to see me.

I only realized I'd been digging my nails into his hands when my body began to relax, his hold on me softening, releasing my wrists, moving to hold me close as we slid off the bed and onto the floor, our bodies touching, our lips a breath apart.

15

"When do you want to show her?" Gabriel asked. He and Syn sat in the library looking at the damning evidence that would leave no doubt in Evangeline's mind as to what Arthur's intention had been.

Syn leaned back in his chair and ran a hand through his hair. "Not sure. She's not remembering on her own, or at least if she is, she isn't telling us."

Gabriel nodded in agreement. "I talked to Alvarez."

It was early evening and the two brothers sat in the library drinking whiskey.

"What does he want?"

"Evangeline. He wants to take her into custody, force her testimony. I don't think either of us thought he didn't know who the thirteenth girl was, did we?"

Syn shook his head. "No, he knew. He's not a stupid man, but I'm not handing her over," Syn said tipping back his glass and swallowing the contents before taking up the bottle to pour another.

"I wasn't suggesting that," Gabriel said, looking at Syn. "I don't trust him any more than you do. You have feelings for her." It wasn't a question. He knew. He knew his brother well enough to see what was happening here.

"No more and no less than you, brother."

And Syn knew him. He swallowed his drink and held out his glass for a refill. "I told Alvarez to give us some time with her. We'd get her to testify."

"And?"

"A week."

"What? A fucking week? She hasn't even come to terms yet with the fact that her fiancé smuggles women to sell, much less that he planned on murdering her, and he wants us to get her ready to testify in a fucking week?"

"Let's give it a few days, figure out how we want to handle it. How did it go with Clara?" Gabriel didn't miss Syn's smile.

"Good. Eva is sweet and submissive. She's resting now. I told her we'd be up to collect her for dinner."

Gabriel nodded and checked his watch, rising. "I'm going to call and check in on Laney. I don't think we can leave Evangeline unprotected and make the trip to see her this week."

"I agree. You know, there hasn't been a change with Laney in the last two years," Syn said.

Gabriel shook his head though. "No, Syn." It was all he said, all he ever said.

Laney was in a vegetative state and there had been no change for a long time. If they pulled the plug on the machines, she would die. Gabriel knew what he would want if it were he lying unconscious on a hospital bed, but he wasn't ready for that yet. Not for his sister. She may have left this world a long time ago but he wasn't yet prepared to let her go. Knowing she was still alive, even in the state she was in, gave him not quite comfort, but something else. It wasn't hope either. That he'd lost a long time ago.

It was simply knowing that she was there, even if she didn't even look like the Laney he remembered anymore.

༺ཽ༻

IT WAS GABRIEL WHO CAME TO COLLECT ME FOR DINNER. I WAS dressed in a floor length champagne-colored silk gown with a halter-top and a plunging neckline with high-heeled sandals to match. I was closing the second strap of the sandal around my ankle when he arrived wearing a tuxedo. All I could do was stare when I saw him. His face was almost smooth, the stubble along his jaw line neater, his dark hair trimmed. When he looked me over from head to toe, he smiled.

"You look beautiful," he said, coming to me and holding out his hand.

I took it and rose to my feet. "Thank you. So do you." As soon as I said it, I looked away, embarrassed. "I mean... you look handsome. A long ways from the man I met that first night on the truck."

He nodded. "Are you ready?"

"Yes." Somehow, I felt at ease. It made no sense but I'd given up on things making sense somewhere during the last few days.

Gabriel led the way downstairs to an extravagantly lit dining room where Syn waited, also dressed formally, also looking beautiful, his dark hair combed back, his face shaved clean.

"Eva," he said, pulling up my chair. "You look lovely."

"Thank you." I sat down cautiously. From the way the

brothers watched me, it seemed I wasn't the only one who was fully aware of the plug inside my bottom.

Gabriel poured wine and we all waited to be served by Caroline and Thomas. It was strange sitting like this around the elegant table eating a delicious roast and talking. Just talking.

"Were you born here? Did you grow up in Mexico?" I knew we were in Mexico from what I'd seen during my transport to the house. I also knew we were in a very isolated spot on a large plot of land, but that was all. The brothers spoke perfect Spanish without a hint of an accent, but they also spoke perfect English, at least to my ears.

"Our mother was from here, our father was American. We were both born in the states. Laney too."

Both Syn and I studied Gabriel as he quieted for a moment.

"Tell me about her."

He hesitated and Syn waited for him to respond. "She was a brat for a long time," Gabriel said, smiling, the look in his eyes making it clear that he was picturing her as that child he remembered. "Always followed us around, getting us into trouble when we would tell her to bug off."

"She'd always want us to play Barbie with her," Syn added.

Gabriel shook his head. "I hated that."

"I know. At least you got to be Ken."

"Well, I *am* the more masculine of the two of us," Gabriel said before turning back to me, his face serious again. "She was a great girl, smart, kind, pretty. Innocent. What happened to her shouldn't have happened."

"I'm sorry it did," I said. "It shouldn't happen to anyone and I imagine seeing her like she is now only reminds you of all you lost, both of you."

Gabriel studied me, then looked down at his plate and nodded once. "What about you? You're an only child?"

"Yes. Mom and dad had trouble conceiving so they had me late. My dad was in his forties when I was born and my mom in her late thirties. I missed not having siblings but my parents were great. My mom passed away when I was ten years old in a car accident and it's been my dad and me ever since. Well, and our extended family, but my dad and I have a pretty close relationship. I can't imagine what he's going through right now, actually." I put my knife and fork down and wiped my mouth, not feeling very hungry anymore. "Will I ever see him again?" I asked point blank. I needed to know their plans. At this point, I didn't think they'd hurt me. I knew it, in fact. But I didn't understand their intentions either. Not hurting me and helping me were two very different things and I didn't understand. Were they truly concerned for my safety? This wasn't about sex. I mean, look at them — two gorgeous, wealthy men. They could have women falling at their feet if that was what they wanted. Why did they want me?

"You'll see your father again, Evangeline. I promise."

I knew he'd keep his promise.

"Then I guess I don't really understand what you can gain from keeping me. If it's not money you want, then what is it? Aren't I more a liability than anything else?"

The brothers looked at each other for a moment, then at me, just as the two girls came to clear the table and Caroline followed them carrying a gorgeous, tall chocolate cake.

GABRIEL FOLLOWED EVANGELINE UP THE STAIRS TO HIS SUITE

of rooms with Syn a few steps behind. She stumbled on her high heels and he smiled, catching her.

"Did you drink too much wine?" he asked, his arm firm around her as he opened his bedroom door.

"I drank what you poured for me," she said, pausing in the narrow doorway, their bodies so close, they almost touched. Her eyes shone and she smiled, her gaze hungry on his mouth as her fingers traveled upward, her small hands easing over his biceps. She paused there, then turned her pretty green eyes up to his, leaned into him as she rose up on tiptoe and kissed him.

It took him by surprise, and, for a moment, he stood still while her lips touched his. He caressed the curve of her low back, fingertips light on her bare skin. She felt so small, so fragile, and as tentatively as she had touched her lips to his, he kissed her back, the connection soft, erotic.

Gabriel leaned back to look down at her flushed face, her swollen mouth, her seduction of him making him want to take his time, to taste every inch of her, to make love to her. He couldn't remember having felt this way before. He fucked women; he didn't make love to them. Yet here she stood, their little captive, her innocent eyes wide on his, waiting.

Her pulse beat rapidly at her neck and she licked her lips. His gaze traveled lower to the nipples that peaked from behind the silk of the dress and he grazed one with the back of his hand, making her gasp. Syn cleared his throat from behind them and Gabriel gently nudged Evangeline into the room. She turned, taking in the large four-poster bed with the mirror that hung from the wall over the headboard. As she walked toward it, Gabriel slid the short zipper of her dress down and undid the buttons that closed at the back of her neck. She stood at the foot of the bed, her eyes locked on his in the mirror, the three casting a striking reflection. Gabriel let the dress fall, the soft silk slipping down to the floor, leaving Evangeline naked before them.

Sliding his jacket off his shoulder and unbuttoning his shirt, Gabriel remained inches from her, kissing the side of her face, the delicate bone at her jaw, the back of her neck, her shoulder, all while pulling his shirt off.

SYN JOINED THEM, TAKING HER WHOLE MOUTH AT ONCE, HIS kiss charged. Her mouth would be his tonight while Gabriel claimed her ass.

He looked down at her, at her glossy eyes that had darkened with arousal, her small hands coming to his bare chest, his shoulders, her hungry gaze on his muscled body. He took her chin in his hand and tilted her face upward, kissing her again. He couldn't get enough of her, tasting her, nipping at her lip, then tweaking her nipple before leaning down to take it into his mouth and sucking it hard. She shuddered, leaning over him as he drew out her hardened nipple with his teeth. He knelt before her then, Gabriel guiding her legs wider, supporting her from behind.

"I like your bare pussy very much, Eva," Syn said, pulling her lips wide, exposing her swollen clit, looking at her wet, waiting sex before licking the length of her slit only to return to that swollen nub. She put her hands on his shoulders but Gabriel took them behind her and held them there, supporting her as he lifted one of her legs over Syn's shoulder.

Eva gasped, losing her balance for a moment, perhaps not yet not trusting that they would hold her. But Gabriel held tight while Syn sucked her clit hard, sliding a finger into her dripping sex.

※

I WOULD HAVE FALLEN HAD GABRIEL NOT BEEN BEHIND ME, giving me his weight, his strength, his powerful body to lean against. My breath was ragged and I wanted my hands free to pull Syn closer to me, to make him suck me harder when he teased. As his fingers slid into my pussy, Gabriel raised my arms to wrap around the back of his neck and lifted my standing leg to lay it across Syn's shoulder so that I was fully supported by the brothers. He pushed the hair off my shoulder and when he used his teeth on my neck, I began to tremble and moan and ride Syn's mouth, grinding myself against his face while Gabriel pinched my nipples hard making me cry out as I came. I closed my eyes and leaned back into Gabriel, squeezing my thighs around Syn's neck, wrapping my legs tight, pulling him hard against my pussy, squeezing every bit of pleasure from my orgasm. Slowly, the waves passed, my breath quieted, my legs softened and I felt myself lifted by powerful arms and laid on the thick, soft comforter of the bed.

I watched the brothers watch me, their eyes hungry. Syn rose to his feet, wiping the back of one hand over his mouth. They stripped off the rest of their clothes while I watched, recovering, unable to decide which body was more beautiful, which man I wanted more — because I wanted them both. I needed them both. I wanted their mouths on me, their hands wandering my body, their cocks inside me.

And I wanted them both at once.

"Turn over on your hands and knees, Evangeline," Gabriel commanded. "Show me your ass."

There wasn't a moment of hesitation as my clit began to throb again, wanting again, and I turned over onto all fours, spreading my knees wide, hollowing my back to give them a full view of my most private parts, wanting them to see me, to touch me. I watched in the mirror as Gabriel approached and placed one hand on my hip before gripping the base of the plug with the other. He then met my eyes in the mirror.

"Did you come all over my brother's face?" he asked, slowly beginning to twist the plug.

"Yes." I barely breathed.

"Are you going to suck his cock now like he sucked your clit? Are you going to open wide and take him deep into your mouth, your throat?"

I nodded, already licking my lips when Syn knelt on the bed in front of me, his cock inches form my face. "Yes. Yes, please."

The brothers smiled and Gabriel twisted the plug, slowly fucking my ass with it.

"You want Syn's cock in your mouth now, don't you? You want him to fuck your mouth while I fuck this tight little virgin ass?"

Syn had come closer, allowing me a taste of his cock before taking it away, stroking it, watching me while one hand caressed my hair as if I were a pet. His pet.

"Ask us, Evangeline. Ask Syn for his cock, tell him how you want it," Gabriel continued, now taking the plug all the way out and leaving my back for a moment to retrieve what I assumed was lubricant from the nightstand drawer. The bed shifted with his weight when he returned, kneeling behind me. He patted my bottom twice, small spanks.

"Your bottom hole is nicely stretched," he said squeezing out a generous amount of lubricant at the top of my ass. "Do you miss it, do you miss the plug?"

Theirs To Take

"Please," I begged, reaching with my mouth for Syn's cock which he kept just out of reach. I wanted them to touch me; I felt cold without that touch.

"Tell us what you want, Evangeline. Tell Syn you want his cock in your mouth and tell me you want mine in your ass. Tell me you want me to fuck your virgin asshole hard."

"Please... I want your cock in my mouth. Please let me have it." Syn let me have one lick, even allowed me to wrap my lips around its head for a too brief moment. I turned to look behind me as Gabriel's fingers began to work lubricant in and around my asshole. I moaned when his other hand touched my clit. "Please fuck me. Please fuck my ass, Gabriel. Please fuck it hard and come inside me. Come inside my ass while Syn comes down my throat. Please... I need you."

The brothers were pleased by that, by my begging. Syn gripped a handful of hair gently and turned my head, offering me his cock slowly as I felt the head of Gabriel's at my asshole. I panicked for a moment, wondering how something so large, so thick, so long would fit inside me there, but it was as though they knew what was going on in my mind and Syn petted me again, gently, reassuringly while Gabriel took hold of my ass cheeks and pulled them wide.

"You can take it, Evangeline. You're nicely stretched, just relax and you can take my cock in your ass. It will hurt a little but I promise it will feel good by the time you're open and ready for me to fuck you."

Gabriel pushed a little deeper then and I made a sound as my bottom tightened, refusing him. "I can't. It's too big," I began, trying to pull away.

"Look at me, Eva," Syn said, turning my face up to his.

I did because I had to.

"You can do it, you can take his cock in your ass, I promise. Keep your eyes on me and push against him. Push against his cock."

"I..." Tears filled my eyes at the painful stretching, but I continued to look at Syn who waited patiently for me to calm while his brother took more of my ass, stretching me, pulling out a little, then pushing in again, pain and pleasure mingling again, seemingly always with the brothers.

"Half way in, Evangeline. You're doing so well. Your ass is so tight and hot around my cock. That's it, push."

He took my clit between two fingers now as he began to claim the inches more aggressively, hardly giving me time to adjust, but I pushed my hips higher to him, not wanting him to stop, wanting him inside me even through the burn.

"That's it Eva," Syn said.

Pre-cum glistened on the tip of Syn's cock and I watched him watch my ass being fucked, the look on his face making me want him more.

"Syn," I whispered.

He looked down at me, smiling, wiping away a tear with his thumb.

"I want you. Let me have you."

He obliged and when I opened my mouth to take his cock, Gabriel pushed in to the hilt, the thrust making me cry out.

"Shh." Syn petted my head again as Gabriel settled inside me, his thighs touching the backs of my legs as he ground a slow circle inside me, his fingers just touching my clit. The sensation was different, tight but good. It hurt a little and I wasn't sure I could take him fucking me hard, but I wanted him, and as his grinding turned into a slow pumping in and out, his fingers still massaging my clit, I wanted him to fuck me. I wanted him to fuck me hard. I wanted to come with Gabriel's cock inside my ass.

Syn moved one hand to my hair and tightened his grip.

"Are you ready to get fucked now, Eva?" he asked. "Are you ready for me to fuck your mouth while Gabriel fucks your ass?"

I nodded, hungry for them, hungry to feel them move inside me, to take and claim me roughly, to come in both my mouth and my ass at once. As Syn slid his cock into my mouth, holding me so that I was angled just right and he could fuck my mouth, Gabriel began a slow thrusting, beginning to fuck my ass. My first orgasm came fast and hard, and the instant I felt my muscles begin to throb around Gabriel's cock, he began to fuck me, to really fuck me and with one cock in my mouth and one in my ass, I lost myself between them, coming and coming, one orgasm on the heels of another. Finally, when I thought I would die from sensation, I felt them both throb inside me, Syn's cock pushing deep into my throat even as tears slid from my eyes, Gabriel's final hard thrusts into my ass, his cock swelling even larger. Thick, warm cum shot into me, down my throat and in my ass, and I knew, as I took all that they gave me, that this was what I would always want.

I would always want them, both of them together, fucking me, using me, making me theirs, giving me pleasure I'd never before thought possible.

16

It was the same dream. I was dancing with Arthur wearing that now ratty silk dress, my hair already out of the beautiful chignon the hairdresser had made, the dirt and scrapes on my arms already there. Arthur had a gleam in his eyes. There was a wicked, evil, crazed shine to them, and closer than before stood Gabriel and Syn, wearing white tuxedos, watching. I looked at my left hand, all scraped, the fingernails chipped and broken, but there was the engagement ring Arthur had given me, back on my finger.

Arthur spun me around, his grip on me tight, and it was as though my hands were glued to his shoulders because I couldn't pull them away. My neck hurt where I knew I'd been pricked by that needle and I wondered if that was why I couldn't talk now.

I looked over Arthur's shoulder at the brothers who stood watching, their faces hard, their eyes never leaving mine. I wanted to call out to them, I tried to, but although I opened my mouth, no sound would come. I knew it was a dream, but I was no less terrified for it. Arthur was hurting me, Arthur had hurt me and I knew it, and he spun me faster and faster so that he took me farther and farther from my protectors.

We were out of the ballroom then and out into the dark night. The stench of farm animals overwhelmed me but Arthur just kept dancing me. I wanted to tell him to stop, to let me go, but I couldn't make a sound and the feeling of dread was so strong, I could almost feel its physical presence. Then finally, abruptly, I was out of his arms. I fell to the ground, his hand catching my left one, and as I watched, men gathered around behind him, Jamison and someone else I didn't know. Arthur said something but I didn't know what it was. They all started laughing then while they watched me struggle to get away, but he held on to me, at least he did until his fingers closed around my engagement ring and he tore it from my finger before dropping me. Arthur stepped back then eyeing the precious stone while the others came, hauling me to my feet, their grips painful on my arms as they pulled me up. That was when I saw the women loaded on the truck, and when they tried to load me, my scream woke me, leaving me sitting upright on the bed, drenched in my own sweat.

I looked around the room. I was alone and daylight poured in around the curtains. My heart hammered in my chest and I rubbed my eyes. It had been a dream. A terrible dream. I was still in Gabriel's bed. I was safe.

"Evangeline!" Gabriel burst into the room followed by Syn, the shock on top of the dream nearly making me scream again. They looked at my face as I stared at them, the warmth and concern I saw in their eyes a sweet relief from the terror of the dream.

Syn came to sit on the bed beside me and pulled me into

his arms, hugging my face against his still naked, wet chest. He smelled as if he had just come from the shower.

"It was nothing. A dream," Gabriel said.

Syn's hand wrapped around the back of my head and held me while Gabriel's weight shifted the bed.

"More like a nightmare?" Gabriel asked, rubbing my back.

I pushed back, nodded and wiped my face, looking at them. Gabriel was dressed in a business suit. Aside from the other night, I'd only seen him in casual clothing.

"Are you going somewhere?" All I could think was that I didn't want to be alone. I didn't want them to leave me.

He nodded. "I have a meeting this afternoon, we both do, but we'll be back before dinnertime. What was the dream?"

I glanced at the clock. The time was half past nine.

"What time do you have to go?" I didn't want to answer their question yet. I needed to think. I needed to figure this out. It was a dream, a nightmare. That was all.

"We leave within the hour." Then, as if reading my hesitation, he added, "Why don't you have a shower then come downstairs. There's something you need to see." The brothers exchanged a long, somber look.

I didn't want to ask what that something was. I knew. Once I saw what they wanted me to see, there would be no going back. Dreams were one thing, but this would be something else entirely and I knew once I saw, I wouldn't be able to hide from the truth any longer.

I knew that was what I was doing. I was burying my head in the sand like a coward.

I needed to think and so I nodded and they left me alone.

If I counted meals, it had been three days since I'd left

Gabriel's bedroom. It seemed as though no one wanted to spoil what was happening, this intimacy that had come out of something so terrible and enveloped us all. But I knew it wouldn't last. I couldn't explain my own feelings, what was happening to me, but there was something there, something powerful.

Something safe.

But it wasn't time for that now. I had to remember what had brought me here; but even so, I was conflicted. It wasn't as though I was still desperate to hold on to the past; I knew in my heart Arthur had hurt me, but I wasn't ready for that truth. It was too terrible to contemplate.

I did know one thing though. I knew that Syn and Gabriel were not evil. That I knew as surely as I knew myself. I had to face what was happening — I just wasn't sure I was strong enough to do it. But what gave me courage was the knowledge that they wouldn't make me face it alone. That they would keep me safe between them.

After my shower, I found a pretty summer dress lying on the bed and slipped it on before going downstairs to find the brothers. We'd talk this out. I had to think of my father too, of how he must be hurting. It was time to face the world again — no matter how much I wanted to hold on to this most unlikely safe haven.

Gabriel and Syn were waiting for me in the library. The first thing I noticed as soon as I walked inside was the newest addition to the furniture there. The armchairs they used had been rearranged somewhat, making room for a new piece. It was a pretty wing back chair, old fashioned, perhaps antique. The color and design were very feminine with large crimson flowers woven throughout the cream-colored upholstery. It was low to the ground with a dark wooden frame to match the rest of the wood in the room.

"Do you like it?" Syn asked.

I touched it, running my fingers over the back of it, realizing it was for me. A gift. "It's very pretty."

They smiled.

"Have a seat," Gabriel said as Syn held out a steaming cup of tea for me.

I took the offered cup and sat down, the heat of the tea comforting.

"It's time you told us about the dream, Evangeline."

Part of me still resisted telling it, resisted speaking the words aloud. The fear was still so powerful, but I knew it was time.

"You're both in it, wearing white tuxedos like white knights." I glanced up at them, my small laugh sounding nervous. "I'm wearing the gown I'd worn that night it all happened, but in the dreams, it's torn and in each dream, it becomes more and more filthy." I brought the cup to my mouth, but didn't sip. "In this one, I could even smell the animals, like on the truck."

It was almost a physical thing, that smell, still as real and as awful as it had been that night. I wanted to drink my tea but my throat had grown tight. I didn't want to do this. I couldn't. Not yet.

I set the cup down harder than I intended and tea splashed out of it onto the coffee table.

"My head hurts." I stood, rubbing my temples.

"Sit down, Evangeline. You need to do this and you need to do it now." Gabriel's stern tone was back, the one I'd not heard from him during the last few days. It was the tone of voice that made me take notice.

I shook my head. "I'm sorry, I can't. Not yet."

Gabriel watched me in silence, his gaze searching mine.

It was as though he was reading my mind, and his eyes told me he'd had enough of my hiding.

Syn stood, as if anticipating my imminent attempt to escape the room.

"I said sit down," Gabriel repeated. "Time's run out."

I turned toward the door, knowing they wouldn't allow me to leave but needing to be made to stay. Needing to fight.

"If you take a step, Evangeline, I promise you, I will get the strap."

I looked at him again and I had no doubt he'd take the strap to my ass. But in a way, I needed him to.

I took that step and from the corner of my eye, I saw Gabriel rise as Syn caught hold of my ponytail, hauling me backward.

"Ow!" I stumbled while he dragged me to Gabriel's desk. Gabriel slid open one of the drawers, drawing out the dark length of a leather strap. "No!"

Struggling was futile, I knew it, but I needed to do it. Syn pushed me forward, bending me over the desk, pressing my belly and breasts to the cool surface, catching both of my wrists in one of his hands. He turned my face to the side and kept his hand on my head so I could watch Gabriel walk calmly behind me.

"No more running," Gabriel said, pushing the skirt of the dress up over my back and roughly taking my panties down to just beneath my hips. "I'm sorry to do this, but I think you need it."

He struck hard, the leather like fire. "Ahh! I don't... God... I don't... need... it."

One big hand flattened upon the small of my back, forcing my hips higher as he continued to strap me.

"This is going to be quick and to the point, Evangeline. Time's run out and I mean that. This isn't just about you anymore. Let me know when you're ready to listen, to really hear."

That was all he said as he strapped me. I cried, struggling against them, trying to break free of Syn's grip, knowing there would be no chance for it. My bottom burned but he kept on punishing me, forcing something from me that I wasn't strong enough to let go of alone. The sounds of leather striking flesh combined with our breathing and my crying, and continued until I'd had enough. Until I stopped struggling. Syn loosened his hold on my wrists and I turned my hands up to hold on to his. I remained prone, as much as I wanted to crawl up and over the desk and run and hide in a corner, I stayed and I took the strokes, ten more like that, each with only a second between them, the thick strap covering the entire surface of my now throbbing ass.

"You ready to listen? To talk?" Gabriel asked from behind me.

I nodded, sniffling, wiping my eyes with the back of my hand.

"Up on your forearms," he said, setting the strap beside me.

I lifted myself up and felt him push my dress higher, his big hand coming to rub one bottom cheek hard before he brought that hand to my hair where he grabbed hold of the ponytail I swore I'd never wear again and hauled me upright. "I do not want to punish you. I don't like hurting you, but this is bigger than you, bigger than all of us, and we're running out of time."

I heard the shuffling of papers near me but closed my eyes when Syn came around and laid them out on the desk where I'd be forced to see.

"Open your eyes, Eva," Syn said.

"You have to face this now, Evangeline. I know it's difficult to find out a man you once thought you loved—"

I turned my head away, or tried to, but Gabriel turned it right back, forcing me to stay, to listen. To finally hear.

"It's difficult to realize a man you thought loved you could have done this to you, to those other women, but Arthur Gallaston is a very bad man and you're the only one who can make sure he never hurts anyone else again."

"Let me go. Please."

"No," Syn said quietly. "Open your eyes."

Open my eyes. I knew I needed to do just that, to see the truth.

"I can't," I said, breaking into a sob, my head hurting from all of it. I thought about what Gabriel said, about those poor women and what would have happened to them if he and Syn hadn't hijacked the truck that night. I thought about my dad. My poor dad who was probably imagining the worst, especially after receiving that package. But when I thought about Arthur, his name only conjured up cruelty and fear. I shivered at the thought of him. There was nothing tender in my memory of him and I wondered when that had changed for me. I'd suspected he'd been having an affair. How naïve of me. If only he'd simply been having an affair.

I gathered my strength and opened my eyes to look at the pages on the desk. There was Arthur standing across the counter at a shop of some sort, something small and dingy. A man smoking a cigarette stood holding my ring in his hand, the engagement ring Arthur had bought for me. I forced myself to turn to the next frame, my throat tight as I tried to hold back my tears. The man kept studying the ring, a different angle of it, and in the next one, he was saying something to Arthur. In the final frame, Arthur had turned his face toward the camera, smiling, tucking an envelope into his pocket.

It was in that moment the memory of that night came back like a flood tide. How I'd followed him to that horrible place, how I'd seen him loading the unconscious women onto the truck, how the other pickup truck had found me hiding, the man tackling me. I remembered Arthur holding the syringe, stabbing my neck with it, pulling away from me when I tried to catch hold of him to break my fall. And finally, Arthur shoving me over with the toe of his shoe, taking the ring from my finger.

I didn't have words then. Somehow, I had known for some time that it was true. That the man I thought I loved stole women and sold them as if their lives didn't count at all. That the man I loved had planned to have me killed, and when that failed, was now exploiting my father's pain to get what he could from him.

Tears came, hot angry tears. I wailed at the world, my screams deafening in the room, my fists flailing at powerful chests, at the two men who could contain me, who would let me rail against them in my acceptance of the truth. There was no mourning in my tears, this wasn't the time for that. That would come, but now, the fire that burned inside me was one of rage, and that fire spread hot through me, giving me strength where I'd once been weak.

Arthur Gallaston would pay for what he'd done and I'd be sure to be the one to collect on that payment.

Gabriel and Syn watched me come apart and they waited, silently, as I came back together again. I looked at them, at each brother in turn, Gabriel and Syn, my protectors. My face felt sticky from all the tears I'd spent, but that was finished now. Gabriel pulled me to him and I pushed my face into his chest, unable to verbalize what I wanted to say as I stood there, allowing myself to be held.

"I'm sorry, Evangeline." He hugged me, rubbing my back hard with one hand and cupping the back of my head with the other.

He dipped his head into the crook of my shoulder and we stayed like that, Gabriel whispering how sorry he was that this was happening to me, telling me it was going to be all right, that they weren't going to let me face this alone. Somehow, I already knew that though. I trusted it. And I was done with tears. He was right, this was bigger than me, bigger than us. I'd been a coward up until now, but no more.

I pulled back, looking up at him. His eyes were soft, filled only with tenderness. He moved his hand to the back of my neck and I felt how small I was next to him, how powerful he was. He'd punished me with those hands, but there was a gentleness there that I'd never known was possible before I'd met him. It was a trust I felt absolutely.

He kissed me then. It wasn't erotic, it wasn't searing with want or need. It was something else, something powerful and fragile all at once, and I kissed him back, wanting that strength, that fragility, that love.

Love.

Was that what this had become?

I turned my head to find Syn watching and I held my hand out to him. He came to me and I kissed him, one hand at Gabriel's chest, the other around Syn's neck, their hands at my back. I kissed Syn hard before turning back to Gabriel and kissing him again, this time with want, with a growing, powerful need. I felt a ravenous hunger I'd never before felt — and I wanted them. I wanted them both again.

Entwined with my lovers, I pulled them down onto the

floor with me, straddling Gabriel, holding him to me, my mouth closing over his. From behind me, I felt Syn, his hands on me, tearing the dress I wore in two, his mouth hot on my neck as he kissed and bit me, pain and pleasure mixing while I devoured — and was devoured by — Gabriel's hot mouth. Gabriel's cock grew hard beneath my hips and without breaking the kiss, I reached for it, opening his pants easily, freeing his length, taking my mouth from his only to bend down and take his cock between my lips instead. From behind me, Syn's hands parted my buttocks and his mouth closed over my pussy, licking, sucking, while Gabriel guided my mouth over his cock. Syn impaled me then, taking me in one hard thrust. Gabriel pulled me up by my hair and closed his mouth over mine as Syn pulled out of my pussy, his hands now pulling my bottom cheeks apart while guiding me over Gabriel's cock, my pussy gaping, wanting to take him inside me, wanting them both inside me.

There was no sound but that of our ragged breathing, our frenzied fucking. This was not love making. This was not soft. This was only need, only taking.

As Gabriel's cock slid into my pussy, Syn's fingers pulled my ass cheeks wider and I felt the wet head of his cock at my asshole. Gabriel leaned me forward a little, just enough to give Syn access to what he wanted. I held onto Gabriel's shoulders, digging my fingers into him, kissing him hard as Syn penetrated my ass. I pushed against him, wanting him deep, wanting him to hurt me, needing the pain. I wanted to come, but I wanted them inside me when I did. I wanted to be theirs and for them to be mine. They'd had me together before, and they'd had me separately, but tonight, tonight was different. Tonight would set fire to the last bridge of the person I'd been before my abduction. It would burn it down into hell, and I wanted nothing but that. I wanted to be free, and at the same time, I wanted to be theirs.

I cried out when Syn pushed hard into me, his cock stretching and filling my ass too fast, the burning pure pain for a moment before he pulled back out and Gabriel drove into my cunt with his thick cock. I moaned as I rode them, Gabriel beneath me, Syn behind, my mouth inches from Gabriel's, my pussy dripping every time he pulled almost all the way out for Syn to take his turn, to fuck my ass. We found our rhythm and the fucking grew hotter, faster, harder, pain and pleasure, fullness, breath and the most primitive sounds human beings can make filled the room. We fucked until I thought I would explode, and finally, I *did*. My orgasm overtook me, so powerful, so all consuming, that it split me in two, waves of sensation washing through my entire body. My pussy gushed, the brothers filling my cunt and my ass with their cum, claiming me as theirs, as I claimed them as mine.

17

A meeting with Alvarez was unavoidable now. They'd put him off for almost two and a half weeks but the man wanted to talk with Evangeline. It was time.

"Are you nervous?" Gabriel asked Evangeline as she twisted her long hair into a braid to the side.

"Yes. Can you tell?"

He smiled and squeezed her hand. "You'll be fine. Remember, he works for the American government. He's our contact to getting the girls to safety after taking down the men and women who buy them, and he wants to put Arthur away. He's on our side."

She nodded, but her eyes betrayed the fact that she wasn't yet convinced. "Why does he need me to talk to him before they arrest him then? I mean, once they arrest him, I can go home. I can talk to him from there."

Gabriel questioned that as well. He and Syn had met with Alvarez and told him she'd testify, told him what she remembered. He should have had enough evidence, but he insisted on meeting with Evangeline in person. "He needs to make sure the evidence is solid, he says. I think he also wants to get a look at you and hear the story from the source. Either way, it will be okay. We'll be there with you every step of the way."

There was a knock on the door and Syn came inside looking Evangeline over and giving her an approving nod. "You about ready to go?"

Gabriel checked his watch. It would be a two-hour drive to the meeting point, a public place they'd agreed upon in case Alvarez decided he'd be better off taking Evangeline with him. Although they'd been working with the man for several years, there was something about him neither was fully comfortable with.

Gabriel nodded. "If we're going to be on time, we'd better go."

Evangeline took a deep breath, smoothing her skirt over her thighs. "Okay. I'm ready."

They went out the door and to the waiting Jeep outside.

"How many cars do you have?" she asked as she climbed into the back seat.

"A few," Syn answered, opening the glove box and setting a revolver inside.

"Wait, why do you have that?"

"Just a precaution. We always have one with us, Eva. Nothing to worry about."

Gabriel's glance in the rear view mirror told him she was worrying. That was fine. Alvarez would be packing too, as would the guards who traveled with him.

They drove out of the gates and onto the long, lonely road that would lead to the highway. The drive was quiet for the most part. Every time he'd glance back at Evangeline, he'd see her looking out the window, worrying her lip. It had been over a month since the kidnapping and she'd been holed up at the house for the last three weeks. She had called her father twice more, which seemed to give her some comfort. But each time, her anxiety returned shortly after the call. She was worried about him, and from the sound of things, he wasn't doing very well. He'd received one more note demanding ransom but he still held strong — or so it appeared. Evangeline wasn't so sure though and Arthur was still in the picture. They had told her she couldn't talk about him to her father. It would be easier to pick Gallaston up if he didn't suspect anything, and Gabriel hoped that would happen later today — right after their meeting.

🐚

We were meeting at a truck stop along the side of the highway. It was busy fortunately, but I seemed to be one of only a handful of women in the place and the truckers took notice. Both Syn and Gabriel carried guns beneath their jackets and stood on either side of me, each with a reassuring hand at my back.

"Which one is he?" I asked as we approached the booth where two men sat. Several stood nearby, watching us intently.

"He's the one with his back to us."

The man facing us looked up and rose to his feet, gesturing for us to slide into the booth. It was then that Alvarez turned around, his gaze falling directly on me.

I stopped short, looking at the fifty-something year old man with graying black hair who now stood to greet us. He wore a suit, an expensive one from what I could see. He looked me over from head to toe and Syn nudged my back, urging me forward the few steps it would take to meet him. I moved.

I don't know how, but I did. My legs were thousand

pound weights, but I walked toward the man and even extended my hand when he reached his out to me. My eyes flitted to the thick ring with the familiar design, but I quickly returned my gaze to his. And when he wrapped my hand in his rough, calloused one, I squeezed Gabriel's, glad he was holding on to me, glad Syn stood to my right, glad they both carried weapons because I knew this man.

That night at the fundraiser when Arthur had received the phone call that had angered him, I'd followed him out of the room as he had excused himself. I'd heard him arguing, something about owing money. I recognized the man whose hand I now shook as the man Arthur been arguing with. Although he'd stood in the shadows and I'd only glimpsed his face for a moment, I recognized his voice, that and the unusual ring I'd seen on his finger when he'd been speaking angrily with Arthur, gesturing with that hand to make some point. This man, whom Gabriel and Syn thought worked with the government, was an associate of Arthur's — in some capacity at least.

And I knew in my heart that he was not one of the good guys.

"Evangeline, this is Javier Alvarez," Gabriel said.

"A pleasure to finally meet you, Ms. Webb," Alvarez said, his voice thickly accented.

My throat went dry but I forced myself to speak. He didn't know I'd seen him that night, I was almost sure of that. They'd been so involved in their conversation that neither he nor Arthur had heard me coming up on them. I had to tell myself that was true. I couldn't think of that night and all it might mean right now. I had to get through this meeting first.

"Nice to meet you, Mr. Alvarez," I managed.

We slid into the booth, Syn and Gabriel flanking me,

Alvarez across from us. Alvarez talked about who he was, what he did for the government. I barely listened to any of it though, my mind racing. What should I do? I knew this man could not be trusted.

I glanced at Gabriel who sat listening, his expression unreadable. Syn's was the same. I wondered if they knew the real truth — or if they too had been fooled by this man. I'd heard them talk about him and had the impression they didn't fully trust him, but maybe that was just how I'd interpreted things? Were they all double crossers? All criminals? Was I the only fool at the table?

I pulled my hands away from both brothers, lacing my fingers together in my lap, feeling a little alone, a lot unsure.

"Gabriel and Syn have told me you remember the night you were taken. I'd like to hear it from you now, Ms. Webb, and once I do, we can move forward with finally bringing Arthur Gallaston to justice. He's been too difficult to catch up until now, but with your testimony, we may be able to put him away for life."

I told him my story. I told it just as I'd told it to the brothers. It was the truth; that was all there was to tell. I couldn't know what this man would do with that truth, but my own plan was beginning to form in the back of my mind. Once he was satisfied with my story, he said he would be in touch to let me know about going home.

JUST OVER AN HOUR LATER, WE WERE ON OUR WAY HOME.

Home. Why did I call it that? I wasn't going home.

I looked at Gabriel and Syn sitting up front talking, more relaxed than they had been when we'd driven to meet Alvarez. I listened to them talk about how this would be over and how Arthur would be put away for good. They said I'd likely see my dad before the end of the week if things went as planned.

I didn't share my own concerns with them. I couldn't. I had been a fool for long enough, first with Arthur and now with them. The way they'd shaken hands with Alvarez, the way he'd patted Gabriel on the back, those few moments when Syn took me to the car and Gabriel remained at the restaurant, he and Alvarez discussing something in hushed tones. I didn't know what the plan was with Arthur and I didn't care. All I knew was that all around me were people I couldn't afford to trust.

I wanted to go home to my dad and I felt guilty that it had taken me so long and that I'd not pushed to be allowed to tell him more, to call him more often. Had I been a puppet to the brothers? A toy? Some sort of sexual conquest? Had I actually considered that I was falling in love with them, these mercenary men? Did Laney, their sister, even truly exist and if so, was she truly lying in a hospital bed kept alive by machines or was that part of their plan to get me to trust them too? To make me have sympathy for them?

I felt alone, so utterly alone.

"You're quiet, Eva," Syn said, smiling at me.

I forced myself to smile back although I had a hard time meeting his dark gaze. "I'm just tired." It wasn't really a lie. I *was* tired. Tired of the lies, the scheming.

"All right. We'll get home and you can take a nap if you'd like. Gabriel and I need to go see Laney today. We haven't been for almost three weeks, so you can have a break from us."

He smiled, that last part meant as a joke. I smiled back at him, hoping it didn't look as forced as it felt.

This was my opportunity, handed to me on a silver platter. The staff had grown to trust me over the last weeks and I'd been allowed to roam freely through the house. When we got back and they left to visit their sister, I would make my escape from this liar's den. I would go home to my father and talk to the police, tell them everything, take care of all of this myself, and then work on forgetting all about Gabriel and Syn.

The thought of that made me sadder than it should, and I shook my head. What a fool I was.

"What's your last name?" I asked suddenly, realizing they had never told me — and I had never asked.

Syn glanced at Gabriel who looked at me in the rear view mirror. They hesitated for a second, and that second confirmed my suspicions.

"Rivera," Gabriel said.

I leaned my head against the window, watching the road. I'd need to remember the way later today. I'd be leaving as soon as they were out of sight.

※

I WENT TO MY ROOM TO TAKE THAT NAP SYN SUGGESTED AND waited for a full hour after they left to make my move. Getting out was easier than I'd imagined it would be. The minimal staff had been told not to disturb me while I rested and I knew Thomas had to go home to tend to something with his family. They trusted me now — or at least didn't believe I would still try to run.

I had watched Gabriel enter in the code to open the gates, and with Caroline busy in the kitchen, I left. I walked out to the garage that housed five of their six cars. The keys to each one hung along the wall by the door and I chose the pickup truck they'd used that first night. Starting up the truck, I drove to the gate. Anxious to be gone, I punched in the code and exhaled a sigh of relief when the gates opened. No longer caring at that point, knowing the brothers would be too far to catch up with me even if Caroline called them now, I drove through the open gate. Driving fast, I programmed the GPS to the city center of Phoenix, Arizona. Eventually, I knew driving in that direction would bring me to a border crossing where I could alert the American authorities.

I'd be safe then.

My optimism was tempered by anxiety though, and I forced myself to focus and drive, the road long and lonely, the time passing by slowly. I was at least making a move. I was no longer a puppet to be manipulated and controlled. My heart hurt at the thought that Gabriel and Syn could have been deceiving me, that everything that had happened in the last weeks might have been a lie. A part of me didn't want to believe it, but I had to harden myself to the possibility. I'd been naïve for so long. I couldn't think about how they'd held me, how they'd been gentle and kind to me.

No, I had to remember their harshness instead, the punishments, the humiliations. It was natural that I'd come to trust them on some level, considering the circumstances. I depended on them for everything and they rewarded me with orgasms the likes of which I'd never experienced before. That's what this was. It had to be. It wasn't natural to fall in love with two men at once, was it? It was my body. It was lust. Nothing more.

※

SYN SAT QUIETLY WATCHING GABRIEL HOLD THEIR SISTER'S

hand and tell her all about Eva as if Laney could hear. Gabriel had always been closer to Laney. Syn had loved his sister too, but he had also mourned her loss. The woman lying on the bed now wasn't Laney, not anymore.

But Gabriel refused to let her go.

Syn hoped that now that Eva was in their lives, maybe she'd make enough of a difference that Gabriel would finally be able to say goodbye. The way he looked now while talking about her, reaffirmed that hope. Gabriel just took longer to do things; it was his way.

He put his hand on Gabriel's shoulder, checking his watch. It was a two-hour drive to the facility and they'd been there for half an hour. He was anxious to get home to Eva. She'd behaved strangely after the meeting with Alvarez. He still remembered when she'd pulled her hand out of his. It wasn't like her and it made him uneasy. The longer they were away from her, the more anxious he became to return to her, to reassure himself that all was well.

"We should go soon," he said to Gabriel.

Gabriel nodded, his eyes still on Laney. "She looks so fragile."

Syn patted Gabriel's shoulder. He had nothing more to say; they'd had this conversation a thousand times.

Syn's phone buzzed in his pocket and he looked at the display before stepping out into the hallway to answer.

"This is Syn."

A frantic Caroline replied. "She's gone, Syn! I came up to bring her something to eat and she's gone."

It took him a moment to register what Caroline was saying, that sudden confirmation of the uneasiness he'd been feeling. "What the hell do you mean *gone*?" Syn spoke angrily into the phone. A nurse down the hall looked up at him and he turned away.

"I'm sorry, Syn. I didn't hear anything and you told us not to disturb her."

"Have you checked the house? Maybe she's in the library?"

"I looked. I searched everywhere. The pickup truck is gone too."

"Fuck!" Syn checked his watch.

"I'm sorry—"

But he'd hung up by then and stormed back into Laney's room.

"Eva's taken the truck. She's gone!"

"What the hell?" Gabriel stood.

"Caroline just called."

"Fuck." Gabriel checked his watch. "Which one?"

"The pickup."

They walked to the door, but Gabriel stopped and turned back. He softly kissed Laney on the forehead, whispering to her. "I love you, sis."

They walked quickly out of the hospital and to their car. Gabriel took the driver's seat while Syn operated the GPS program on his phone. All six of their cars were equipped with a tracking system, so they'd be able to find the truck.

"Pick her up yet?" Gabriel asked

"She's heading toward the border."

§⦁

I LOOKED AT THE TIME, ANOTHER HOUR AND A HALF HAD passed and I wondered if anyone realized yet what I'd done. Well, it didn't matter now. By the time they figured it out, I'd be back home. Arthur would be arrested once I told my story and it would finally be over.

I switched on the radio, not wanting to think about that until I had to.

I knew I was getting closer to the border as traffic began to pick up, and soon, lines started to form for border control. I looked around as I slowed, seeing the others lined up in their cars, a lot of families, mostly Mexican. I'd stand out, I knew that. But without any identification, I wanted to stand out, to draw attention to myself, to help corroborate my story

When the main building came into view, I veered out of the idling line of cars and stopped the truck along the curb. Two armed men quickly came toward the truck before I'd even had a chance to close my door. I held my arms out, palms up to show them I was not a threat.

"I'm an American," I called out. "I was kidnapped and brought here against my will. I want to talk to the American authorities."

They didn't slow their pace as they neared, and when they reached for the large rifles on their backs, I momentarily questioned my decision. They barked in Spanish and pointed to the door of a building where two more men stood guard.

"I'm an American," I said again. "My name is Evangeline Webb, I'm Senator Webb's daughter. I was kidnapped—"

Before I could say anything further, another man came around from behind the advancing guards.

"Let her pass," the man said to the others. He spoke in heavily accented English as he hurried toward me, his gaze intent on me. "Ms. Webb," he said, reaching out a hand to shake mine, looking me over from head to toe. "Are you hurt? We've been looking for you."

They had?

The man introduced himself as Hernandez and ushered me into the building.

"I want to talk to my father. I want you to call the American authorities."

I barely had a chance to look around as he led me through the busy lobby, one hand at my back, a sense of urgency to his step. We passed through several largely deserted hallways and at the very end of a final corridor, he opened a door and gestured for me to go inside. "We'll make those calls as soon as possible. Just let me get you a bottle of water first. I'll be right back. Please, stay here."

I went inside, unsure what I should do, everything happening too fast, part of me questioning why he wasn't asking more questions. I started to wonder if I'd made a mistake, but I stayed put, looking around the room. I sat at one side of a large desk, an empty chair on the other side. There was a mirror on one wall. I knew it was a two-way and turned away quickly, feeling less and less sure of what I was doing here. I looked at the clock and sat tight, but when twenty minutes had passed and no one had come, I went to the door, intending to demand that I be allowed to contact the Americans. But when I tried the door, I found it was locked. I tried again, but the doorknob wouldn't turn.

"Hello? I'm an American. I was brought to Mexico against my will. Please let me out of here!"

But no one came. I called out a few more times, banging on the door, but he'd taken me so far from the main office that I wondered if anyone could even hear me. I gave up after a few minutes, feeling suddenly exhausted, wanting to cry, wondering if there was anyone I could trust.

Gabriel drove fast. "She was different after our meeting with Alvarez."

"She said she was tired." Syn rubbed his eyes. "We shouldn't have left her alone."

"Well, we won't once we get her back."

But what if they didn't get her back?

No.

Gabriel wouldn't think of that now. He couldn't.

"Truck's still stopped," Syn said, studying the GPS screen. She's definitely not moving anymore."

"We're still about two hours away. Call our contact. See if he can locate her."

Syn nodded his head. "Already on it, brother."

Ronaldo picked up quickly and Syn spoke, asking about her. He turned to Gabriel and gave him a nod.

"Okay, do what you can to keep her there. We're on our way." He hung up the phone. "She's demanding to call the American authorities, saying she was kidnapped."

Gabriel thought quickly. "It's Alvarez. Something about him spooked her."

"She should have trusted us. Damn it!"

"Well, Hernandez can be bought, brother, as you know. We'll deal with Evangeline when we get her home. Let's just get her there safely first."

"And let's hope we're the ones he contacts first," Syn said.

That concerned Gabriel. Hernandez could be bought, that much was true, but he didn't care much about who was paying him — as long as he was being paid. And as far as they knew, Alvarez had contacts everywhere.

It was more than an hour later when Hernandez opened the door, only giving me a reluctant glance before stepping aside to allow two men to enter followed by Javier Alvarez. I stood, backing away so quickly, I knocked my own chair over.

"I want to call the police," I said over his head to Hernandez.

"Mr. Alvarez is the police," he said.

"We meet again, the lovely fiancée of my good friend," Alvarez said, extending a hand. He shrugged when I refused to take it. "You'll be happy to know that Arthur is relieved we have found you and he is on his way to meet you himself."

"What?" I shook my head, trying to dash around the fallen chair only to have two sets of hands grab hold of my arms.

Alvarez waved a hand at the men who released me immediately. "No need for that now, is there?"

"Arthur did this to me. You can't take me back to him. He'll kill me." Tears filled my eyes, cold dread sinking deep in my belly.

"Come now," Alvarez said, gesturing to the door where Hernandez stood ready to help him. "We shouldn't keep him waiting. If we leave now, we might just make it to the airport before he lands."

"Please don't," I said, struggling against the men who hustled me out of the room and down a corridor. The heat was stifling when we stepped out of the air-conditioned building and into the afternoon sun where an SUV waited for us, its engine idling.

Alvarez opened the back door and one of the men climbed inside, pulling me in with him. The other man went to sit in the front seat. Alvarez slid in beside me, and as soon as he closed his door, we drove off.

"I wondered if you had recognized me," Alvarez said. I flinched when he touched me, pushing the braid off my shoulder.

"Why are you doing this?"

"Why does anyone do anything?" he asked, his softly spoken words deceiving. "Money. Your fiancé owes me a great deal of it and I'm going to help him to pay it back."

"If it's money you want, my family is wealthy. My father can pay."

He shook his head. "No, no sense in involving a sick old man," he said as if he were doing me a favor.

"Sick?"

"You haven't heard? He had a heart attack early this morning. It was just on the news."

"A *heart attack*?" Tears slid down my face.

"Don't worry, he's going to be all right. But I don't want to give him another shock."

"You don't work for the American government, do you?"

He looked shocked at my question. "Oh no, I do. Absolutely. I simply... how do you say it? I have work on the side."

"Work Gabriel and Syn don't know anything about." I realized it as I said it. I'd made a terrible mistake.

He shook his head, that false smile still on his face. "I'm afraid not. Does that disappoint you? I thought it would please you. You have some affection for one of the brothers, after all?"

His words were meant to taunt me — and I refused take the bait.

"Which one is it? Gabriel? Handsome, brooding — what women want, no? Too serious, that one. Still holds on to hope his dear sister will one day wake up." He snapped his fingers, making me jump. "Poof! Like magic."

"Stop."

"No? Not Gabriel? Then it must be Syn." He shook his head. "Headstrong, although he is the more realistic and he does seem to enjoy his work."

I looked away from his predatory grin.

"No, wait, don't tell me," he said, his hand suddenly gripping my knee.

"Don't touch me!"

He held up that hand as if he were innocent, feigning offense. "Is it both of them?"

I forced myself to look at him, to try to find some semblance of humanity in his eyes, but finding none, I turned away.

He shook his head and clucked his tongue. "In love with the Rivera brothers. When they first began to work for me, they were rigid with their rules. But having so many beautiful women about and at their command? Well, let's just say you certainly wouldn't be the first to fall for them."

That hurt me, even though I knew he would say anything *to* hurt me.

"Sad." He pushed a lock of hair behind my ear before I jerked my head away. He sighed and checked his watch, then lit a cigar and puffed on it as we drove in silence to meet Arthur.

SYN'S PHONE RANG. HE LOOKED AT THE DISPLAY TO FIND IT was Ronaldo and he picked up quickly, putting it on speaker.

"Alvarez picked her up and she didn't go willingly."

"Fuck! Which way are they headed?"

"Heard him mention an airport."

"Okay Thanks, Ronaldo." Syn hung up the phone.

"I wonder if Alvarez was the man Gallaston had been talking to when Evangeline walked in on the conversation that night," Gabriel said.

"It makes sense if she recognized him at the meeting. Would explain why she was so reserved."

"So he worked with Gallaston then. She'd said they were arguing over money. Wonder if Gallaston owed Alvarez."

"And our relationship with Alvarez put us on the wrong side as far as Eva was concerned."

"I'm not sure this could get any worse."

"Here," Syn said, stabbing a finger at the GPS screen. "There's an airport about forty minutes from here. It's mostly cargo flights, and it's remote. I bet that's the one he's taking her to. If we're lucky, we'll get there within a few minutes of them."

"All right, give me the directions, brother." Gabriel considered for a minute. "And call in the proper authorities."

Syn nodded. Calling in the authorities meant disappearing off that site before they got there because — officially, anyway — the Rivera brothers were ruthless men who dealt in sexual slavery. Their ties to the American government would be disavowed.

They had no choice though. Eva's safety was what was important now

18

I'd made a terrible mistake. I had been so stupid. Why hadn't I just told Gabriel and Syn about Alvarez? Why did I suspect them? They'd been the good ones from the start, despite the occasional cruelty they'd displayed at the camp. They'd done what they had to do there. If they hadn't lied to us about our futures, it wouldn't have worked. I wondered now how many of those women I had been with truly had been returned home.

Did Gabriel and Syn trust Alvarez blindly? No, I knew they didn't. They had their own misgivings. Why hadn't that been enough for me to trust them when the time had come?

Ever since they'd brought me to their home, they'd taken care of me, treated me as though I were precious. Even their punishments were followed by tender affection. How could I have been so stupid? I couldn't think about what that stupidity might cost me — and those I loved.

My father had had a heart attack. He was probably lying in a hospital bed right now and he needed me. And Gabriel and Syn — they'd know by now. Enough time would have passed that they'd be home and would have found my empty room. I'd left nothing, not even a note. What if they tried to come look for me — and found me? What then? Would they too become casualties of my own stupidity?

We drove off the highway about half an hour later and took a narrow, less maintained road toward the airport. I watched a low flying plane coming in overhead and wondered if it was Arthur.

Arthur. Now that I remembered what he'd done to me, to so many others, what would I do when I saw him again? At that thought, fear began to turn into something else — anger. He'd fooled me, tricked my father, made me believe he loved me — then callously sent me to my death.

His words from that night chilled me now:

Just make sure there's only twelve left on that truck at the drop-off point. You know what to do. No fuck-ups, nothing linking back to me. Otherwise, make it look good...

I was the thirteenth — the one who wasn't supposed to make it. Who wasn't supposed to be alive right here, right now. Except that I was.

"Here we are," Alvarez said as we neared the tall fence that surrounded the airport. I watched the airplane land as our car drove through the open gates. I watched as the doors of the plane opened and Arthur came down the stairs, his dark hair slicked back in its usual style, his suit stylish, expensive, dark glasses shielding him from the sun. He was flanked by two men, one of whom I recognized. Jamison, who was always by his side, and someone else I didn't know. Our car came to a stop some distance from the airplane and Alvarez opened the door and climbed out, holding out his hand for me to follow. I went, but didn't take his hand, and I walked around the SUV to face my fiancé. I hesitated for a moment but forced myself to walk on, my head held high.

"Javier," Arthur said, taking off his glasses, his gaze

sweeping me before he addressed Alvarez. "What a pleasant surprise your call was."

Alvarez's expression didn't change. "I'm here to finish with our business, Arthur."

"I imagine you are," Arthur said, his gaze settling on me, sending a shudder through me. I looked into his eyes then, realizing I felt nothing but loathing for the man. "Evangeline," he said, without even a suggestion of emotion on his face.

"Didn't think you'd see me again, did you Arthur? You fucking bastard."

He raised his eyebrows in mock surprise. "Where's my sweet little fiancée?" he asked, coming closer.

I took a step back only to be grabbed by Alvarez's men.

"Don't touch me," I said to Arthur. "How could you do this to me? To my father? He treated you like his own son!"

His gaze was flat and he had no response. I wasn't surprised. Someone as inhuman as him surely couldn't feel.

"One day, you'll get what you deserve, Arthur."

"One day," he said, chuckling. "But today's not that day." He retrieved a pistol from his pocket and held it casually at his side.

My heart raced. He was right, today wasn't that day and as strong as I might think myself, I stood here helpless between seven armed men who only meant me harm.

The sound of helicopters overhead had us all looking up. That was when the first gunshot rang out. One of the men holding me stumbled with a groan, nearly bringing me down with him as he pitched forward, hitting the tarmac face first. I screamed and the men scrambled to shield themselves from the gunfire raining down upon us as two more helicopters flew into view.

"Evangeline!"

I spun around to find Gabriel and Syn running toward me, guns blazing as more of Alvarez's men poured out from the hangar where they'd been lying in wait.

But I turned away from the brothers. There was one thing I had to do.

Taking the gun from the hand of one of the fallen men, I raised it to where Arthur stood shielding himself beneath the wing of the plane, firing his weapon.

"Evangeline, no!" Gabriel called out from behind me.

With trembling hands, I aimed my weapon, readying it.

"Arthur!" I called out. I wanted him to see me. I wanted to look him in the eye when I did it. I wanted him to know it was *me*.

At first, when he turned to me, he looked surprised — then pissed off. I fired just as he aimed for me, the shot throwing him backward. He recovered quickly though, turning toward me again with hate in his eyes.

More shots rang out, the sound deafening. Arthur raised his revolver, an evil grin on his face, but before I could get another shot off, he fell backward.

"No!" He was mine. I wanted to be the one to make him pay!

"Eva!" Syn called out.

I turned to them to find Gabriel lowering his weapon. I wasn't finished though. I ran toward Arthur who was lying on the ground. He wasn't dead yet, but before I could get another shot to finish the job, something hit me, hard, and searing pain exploded in my chest, sending me to the ground in agony.

"Eva!"

I lay unmoving, stunned, knowing the blood that pooled on the tarmac beneath me was my own.

"Evangeline."

I opened my eyes to find Gabriel kneeling beside me, a pistol in one hand, his other hand on my wound, pressing on it.

"Look at me, Evangeline. Keep looking at me."

"I'm..."

Syn faded in and out from behind him before I felt my head raised and then lowered again onto something soft. His lap.

"No, Eva! Do not close your eyes! Look at me. Fuck!"

"I'm sorry..."

"Don't you dare fucking die! Don't you dare!"

"Get a medic here, damn it!"

I couldn't tell who was speaking anymore, Syn or Gabriel, or was that Jamison? I opened my eyes once more to see Alvarez lying face down less than fifty feet from me. I knew he was dead. Was I dead? Was I dying?

"Eva!"

I tried to open my eyes again. They kept repeating my name, telling me to look at them, but I couldn't open them. I just... I had to... sleep.

19

"You waking up, honey?"

I blinked, trying to adjust to the bright overhead lights. Someone squeezed my hand and I turned my head in that direction, blinking again, trying to focus on the blurry, but familiar face smiling down at me.

"Dad?"

His smile widened and a tear slid down his cheek.

"It's me, honey. You're in the hospital back home."

"What happened?" I asked, remembering. "Gabriel and Syn…"

"Who?"

"Gabriel and Syn. They helped me."

"If you're talking about that son of a bitch Alvarez, he's dead. And Arthur's in jail where he'll rot."

I shook my head. "No… I mean…"

"You were extremely lucky the bullet that hit you just missed your heart. You're probably feeling pretty sore, but you're going to be fine. Jamison, Arthur's right hand man, was working undercover for the DEA. He tipped off the authorities to your location when Alvarez decided to hand you over to that son of a bitch. Sounded like gunfire had already broken out when they got there and you were shot early on. Alvarez was killed and Arthur arrested."

"Jamison works for the DEA?"

"They'd been on to Arthur for some time, but until now, they had nothing to nail him with."

"But Syn and Gabriel, they helped me. They were the ones who saved me in the first place, saved all of us. If it hadn't been for them..."

My dad shook his head. "Those names don't ring a bell, honey, and I've read the reports backwards and forwards. You've been through a lot, maybe it's the trauma..."

No, it wasn't the trauma.

The door opened and an older nurse walked in. "Now, Senator, aren't you supposed to be sitting down in that chair?"

My dad's face lit up when he smiled at her. It had been much too long since I'd seen that look. "Now, now, Addy. No need to get feisty," he said, lowering himself down.

It was then I remembered he'd had a heart attack. "Dad, oh my God, how are *you*?"

He smiled. "Well, we're sharing a room," he said, pointing to the other hospital bed.

I chuckled.

"He snores, honey. I'll try to get you out of here fast," Addy said, casting a flirtatious glance toward my dad. "Now let's have a look at you."

20

For one full year after that day, I moved back into the house I'd grown up in. I had interview after interview with detectives and prosecutors and Arthur was finally behind bars for good. That was the first big hurdle and I found I had no feelings left for him at all. He was to be punished and it was good. How many lives he had destroyed we would never truly know, but at least it was a sort of closure for his victims, closure for me.

I tried to learn more about the fate of the women who had been at the camp with me, and Lara especially, but all they would tell me was that they were unharmed, which had to be enough.

Weeks and then months went by as I tried to find out what had happened to Gabriel and Syn. The fact that Jamison was a good guy blew my mind. But I didn't dwell on the fact — I was grateful to be alive, and home, even though I missed the brothers. The notion that they didn't want to be found weighed heavily upon me. I knew their activities weren't entirely on the up and up, but they had to know I didn't care about that. I owed them an apology and a thank you, at the very least. They had risked their lives to save mine. But that wasn't the only reason why I searched for them now.

Addy came around often with the excuse of checking up on my dad or myself. It was fun to watch them flirt and I was happy to see my dad look at a woman like that again. It had been so long since my mom had died that I'd forgotten he could still feel those kind of emotions. It was nice. Now that he was doing so well, it was time for me to pick up where I had left off a year ago.

It was late afternoon when I headed to the coffee shop to meet Jamison. I hadn't had contact with him in the last year, not until a few weeks ago. I knew he was the link between Gabriel, Syn, and Arthur. He was the informant who had tipped them off to the cargo, to my being on that truck. He was also the one who had sent the evidence of Arthur's betrayal to Syn. And he had agreed to meet with me.

I checked my watch as I pulled into the parking lot of the busy café. I was early, but when I went inside, I found Jamison already sitting in a booth at the very back. A mug of coffee stood on the table in front of him, but his eyes were on the door, and when he saw me, he greeted me with a short nod.

I slipped into the booth across from him and smiled. "Thank you for agreeing to meet with me." It was still strange to be here with him. I couldn't shake the memories of him always in the background, always near when Arthur was there.

"I figure I owe you one," he said. I knew he referred to the night of the kidnapping. They had been pretty rough with me and he'd had no choice but to stand back and let it happen. It was either that, or blow his cover.

"I don't blame you for anything," I said, wanting to make that clear.

"Would you like a cup of coffee? Something else perhaps?"

"No, thanks." I studied him, wondering how forthcoming he would be. "Have you talked to them?" As soon as I asked it, the guise I'd adopted for my father's sake fell away, and the happy, confident face I'd worn for the last year gave way to the truth. I felt vulnerable, I felt sad, and as strong as I tried to appear to be for my father's sake, inside all I wanted was to see them again.

I missed the brothers. I missed them so much.

I knew from the way Jamison looked at me, that he saw it too.

He nodded.

"How are they?"

"Reasonable."

They had sold the house half a year ago but I knew it had been emptied long before then. I had looked, I had searched, but the Rivera brothers and all of their staff had disappeared.

"Do they… ask about me?"

He studied me intently as if weighing his thoughts, measuring what he could, what he *would* tell me. I had to remember this was a man trained to keep secrets.

"Ms. Webb," he said, leaning forward, exhaling. "It would be best if you were to forget about what happened, and move forward with your life. You're young. You can start fresh. This is an opportunity most don't get. Forget the past."

"Is that what they said? Have *they* forgotten the past?" Hot tears filled my eyes. I took a tissue out of my bag and twisted it in my hands. "Have they forgotten me?" I swiped at the few tears that fell down my cheeks, my hands shaking.

He looked beyond my shoulder for a moment, his expression at first softening, then hardening again. "I've had contact with them twice in the last year. They've asked about your well-being during each of those visits."

I would take that. I would take any little bit of hope. "I just want to see them one more time. I need to…"

He shook his head and looked away, and for a moment I feared he would walk out. I reached out and took hold of his forearm with both hands, determined to keep him here.

"Please. They left the house and I can't find anything about them at all. They just… disappeared. I want, no, I *need* to see them one more time. You're the only one who can help me. Please."

I held onto him. He was my last hope and I knew it.

Jamison glanced at where I held onto him before returning his gaze to mine. I placed my hands back on my lap. He called the waitress over and asked for a pen. Once she had left, he turned a coffee stained napkin over and scribbled down an address, then slid the napkin over to me.

"This was the last address I had. They've moved twice though so I can't be sure if they're still there. They've now cut off all ties with the government."

I picked up the napkin, memorizing the address, recognizing the name of the small California town.

"Thank you," I said, smiling up at him. "Thank you so much."

"I hope you find what you're looking for," he said, rising to stand. "Goodbye, Ms. Webb."

"Goodbye, Mr. Jamison." As I watched him go, I realized that wouldn't have been his real name. But it didn't matter anymore.

I left a few minutes after he did, heading home to book my flight.

My flight landed at Santa Barbara's small airport in the early evening the following day. I picked up my rented Jeep, programmed the address and drove up along the coast to where I hoped Gabriel and Syn still lived. I realized there could be a chance they were gone but I wouldn't allow myself to think about that. Not yet. I had a lead, finally. And I had hope.

It was nearly a two-hour drive and the last part of it was over an unpaved, private road. Just like them, I thought. The sun was setting when the house finally came into view. The location alone was breathtaking, but with the purples and deep, burnt orange of the sky, it was almost otherworldly. Tucked into the mountains on a wholly private piece of land and surrounded with lush gardens. The house, although not the massive mansion I'd known in Mexico, was still quite large and typical of the architecture of the other homes in the area.

And I should have expected the gate.

Pulling up as close as I could to the house, I climbed out of the car, walking up to ring the bell. I paused and looked through the gates at the house in the distance. It was completely quiet, no signs of life at all, the windows dark. I pushed the button again and waited. Nothing happened. I tried one more time, wondering if it was even working. I began to doubt myself then, wondering if I'd come all this way only to find a deserted house. I'd come too far to entertain that thought now though. Giving it another few minutes, I looked up at the gate. I could get over it; it wasn't that high. I went back to the Jeep, climbed onto the hood and pulled myself over the gate, landing with a thud on the other side, grateful I'd worn flats today. I stood, wiped at any dirt clinging to my skirt, straightened my hair and headed toward the house.

&

Syn's phone buzzed to life.

"We've got company," he said, checking the alarm that had gone off, alerting them of the intruder.

He and Gabriel had moved into the house six months ago, and in that time there hadn't been any trouble. In fact, since the day they'd signed the contract, they'd had no visitors at all. Gabriel tucked a small pistol into the waistband of his jeans. Although they'd left their past behind, the past didn't always stay away, and given the nature of the business they were involved in, they would forever need to be prepared.

Walking around the house, they took cover and quietly watched as someone walked out of the garden and toward the front steps. Before the intruder got close to the house though, Syn lunged, clamping a hand over the trespasser's mouth, wrapping an arm around her waist, holding her tight to him.

Her.

Syn looked down at the top of her familiar head as she struggled to free herself, saying something against his hand. It was the feel of her body pressed against his, along with her scent that alerted him to who she was.

"What the..." Syn said, turning their guest around.

"Evangeline?" Gabriel said, lowering the arm that held the pistol aimed and ready.

Syn released her and she took a step back, stumbling. He caught and righted her, watching her as she slowly got her breathing under control.

"Did I hurt you?" Syn asked, looking her over from head to toe for any physical signs of damage.

"No," she said, righting her blouse and pushing her hair behind her ears. "It's just... I didn't expect quite that greeting."

"Did it occur to you to ring the bell?" he asked before pulling her in for a tight hug.

She hugged him back hard as her tears began to fall. "I did. Three times," she said, holding him tighter still.

Syn pulled back and looked at her while she swiped the back of her hand over her eyes.

"You scared me," she said.

It was Gabriel's turn to take her into his embrace now and he hugged her tightly. Syn looked at his brother, at how he had closed his eyes as he held her, inhaling deeply as if she weren't real, as if she would disappear at any moment.

"I don't think she can breathe," Syn said.

Eva giggled as Gabriel loosened his hold on her.

"How did you get over the fence?" Syn asked

"I climbed on top of my Jeep and jumped."

"We should look at that bell," Gabriel said, his gaze never leaving hers.

"Eva, how did you find us?"

"Jamison."

Syn looked at Gabriel. Jamison had approached them twice more about jobs, but they'd turned them both down, officially no longer available for work.

"Is it okay? That I'm here, I mean?" Eva asked, her expression, her voice, her body language betraying how uncertain she was.

"Is it *okay*?" Syn asked, running one finger over the inside of her forearm before taking her hand.

Gabriel touched her face, brushing her hair back. "It's more than okay."

They led her inside, none of them talking, the mood suddenly growing more serious.

"Arthur's in jail where he'll stay for the rest of his life," she said once they'd settled in the living room.

They nodded. "We followed the trial." They'd followed more than that. They'd been keeping tabs on her. "You look as though you've healed," Syn said, noting how quiet his brother was, not missing the fact that Eva cast quick, uncertain glances in his direction.

"The bullet had just missed my heart," she said, unbuttoning the top of her blouse, turning around and sliding it down over her shoulder. "I never in my life thought I'd have a bullet wound for a scar."

"How is your father?"

She smiled. "He's doing really well. He and one of the nurses even hit it off, so he's got a girlfriend for the first time since my mom passed away."

"That's good to hear. Evangeline," Gabriel said. "Does anyone else know about this location?"

Syn watched, waiting.

She shook her head. "No. I wouldn't tell anyone, Gabriel. I just... I needed to see you. Both of you." She reached out and took each of their hands in hers. "I owe you both an apology. I doubted you. After all you did for me, I doubted you and even after that, you risked your lives for me." Tears reddened her eyes again. It always softened her face somehow when she cried, her vulnerability making him want to protect her even more. "I wanted to say thank you for everything. You saved my life, more than once."

Syn squeezed her hand, looking at her. "Is that why you came?" he asked, trying not to seem disappointed.

She drew in a deep, shaky breath and the little pulse at her neck beat fast.

"Evangeline?" Gabriel asked when she hesitated.

She looked from one man to the other and shook her head. "This last year, it's been really hard. I feel stronger, surer of myself. I'm no longer my father's daughter — or Arthur's fiancée. I'm me. I've thought about you both. A lot. I thought my feelings would fade, thought things would go back to normal. But they didn't — and things can never go back to the way they were."

She stopped there, looking expectantly, hopefully, at the two of them.

Syn studied her, and, after a moment, Gabriel stood, running a hand through his hair. Syn kept her hand in his. He knew what it took for her to say those words. She was opening herself up to them. He glanced at Gabriel. His brother's gaze was intense as usual, his jaw tight. Syn decided then that he'd kick his brother's ass if he said anything to hurt her.

"We took Laney off the respirators last month," Gabriel said. "She passed away quietly two days later."

Syn knew what he was thinking but he kept silent and watched Eva as she listened.

"In a way, her death closed a chapter for me, for both of us."

Syn nodded when Gabriel looked at him for confirmation.

"But those memories, the knowledge of what we've done to avenge what happened to her, they'll always be a part of us, Evangeline. No matter how much time passes, the things we've done won't fade away and we'll never truly be free of them. You're young. You have your whole life ahead of you."

She glanced at Syn then, understanding what Gabriel

was saying, and pulled her hand out of Syn's. He wasn't sure he agreed with Gabriel. He knew Gabriel had her safety in mind first and foremost, but there was so much more at stake now. For all of them.

"What are you saying, Gabriel?" she asked.

"You're free. You don't have to have the weight of *our* past drag down *your* future. What happened to you, well, it happened and that's already far more than you should have to carry with you. You don't need us, or our past, complicating your life."

Syn watched her expression go from hurt to angry in moments.

"Everyone always thinks they know what's best for me. Well, they don't. *You* don't." She spun, striding away, then turned back again, angrier. "You want to know what's complicated? Trying to pretend that you're fine when you're not, not even close. When you can't even breathe when you think about those days together with just the three of us. Those nights. When you're trying desperately to pretend you're okay but you come up against dead-end after dead-end. When the men you love disappear off the face of the earth. When they leave you alone to make sense of what the hell is going on inside your messed up head." She dropped her head, tears flowing anew. "Your messed up heart."

Gabriel went to her then, but she pushed him away.

"Let me go! You don't care. Neither of you do."

"That's not true, Evangeline. Not even close."

"Eva, we do care. Please, sit down. Please," Syn implored.

It took both of them to finally get her to sit back down.

"Do you mean what you just said?" Syn asked.

She thought about it, looking as though she were going through every word in her head. Then she looked up at them, nodding.

"What do you want, exactly?" Gabriel asked.

"I want you to not make me go. I want to stay here with you. I want it to be like it was those weeks at the house in Mexico."

"What about your father? He's a political figure. This could be a scandal he neither wants nor needs."

"This is his last term. He's retiring. As for him wanting this, he's my father. He wants me to be happy — and I'm not happy. Not now. I'm alone and I can't imagine being with anyone else but you. I love you. Both of you."

"Evangeline," Gabriel began.

Syn put a hand on Gabriel's shoulder to halt his words.

"I want you," she continued, her eyes on Gabriel as she stepped closer, unbuttoning her blouse and slowly sliding it from her shoulders. She pushed her skirt down over her hips and stepped out of it before reaching back to unhook her bra which she dropped on top of the pile. She shifted her eyes from Gabriel's to Syn's as she pushed her panties off. "And I need you," she said, coming to kneel before them in a perfect posture, her knees wide, her hands, palms turned upward, resting on her thighs. "Please," she whispered, her eyes searching theirs, pleading with them before she lowered her lashes and bowed her head.

***

Gabriel looked at her, at how small, how fragile she looked kneeling naked before them exactly as they'd taught her. His chest felt full to the point of pain. He loved her. There was no doubt of that. Hell, he'd known that for a very long time.

Swallowing hard, he laid his hand on the top of her head, holding it there. He'd missed the feel of her thick, soft hair, of intertwining his fingers in it, pulling it. She didn't make a sound as he tugged, turning her face up to his, the tears at the corners of her eyes betraying her pain.

"Clasp your hands behind your back," he said, his voice harder.

She did.

Syn knelt behind her, his hands coming around to cover her breasts before pinching both nipples hard, causing her to suck in a breath. He held tight though, kissing her neck, her exposed throat.

"You want this?" Gabriel asked, tugging harder on her hair as he undid his jeans.

Syn moved a hand down between her legs, taking her clit between thumb and forefinger.

"You want us," Gabriel continued, his thick cock now inches from her face. "Like this, always?" he asked, pressing the head of it to her ready mouth, giving her a taste as Syn moved his other hand behind her. Gabriel knew the instant his brother's finger pressed against her back hole because she rose up a little, taking Gabriel's wrist, not quite trying to free herself, but holding there.

"This is how it will be with us," he continued, neither he nor his brother letting up. "Always. Two Masters to serve, to obey."

"To love," she managed, her voice thick with lust, courage and strength in her steady gaze.

Syn rose to his feet then, giving Gabriel a nod. Gabriel looked down once more at the still kneeling Evangeline and slowly pulled her to her feet. His hand in her hair turned to cup rather than grip and he drew her toward him, kissing her hard. She melted against him, her arms wrapping around his neck, her mouth opening to him.

"I love you," he whispered once, their eyes locked. "Never doubt that."

Their kiss deepened but Gabriel felt the pull when Syn wanted his turn, taking her from him, her mouth having barely left his before Syn's closed over hers and he whispered those same words.

"I love you, Eva."

MY BODY YIELDED EASILY TO THEM AND I COULD NO LONGER tell the difference between their touch. Two sets of hands explored every inch of flesh, my mouth never left unused. From Syn's sensual kiss to Gabriel's fierce one, my eyes opening only in time to see the exchange, to see the powerful bodies of the men I loved bared to me. From one to the other I went, one pinching, the other caressing, pain and pleasure like a sort of duet, an inseparable pair — just like them. This was how it would be with the brothers, always.

I tasted them in turn as they tasted me, leaving no part of me untouched while I lay on the large ottoman, Gabriel in my mouth, Syn with his on my pussy. I felt my throat open as Gabriel's cock filled me deeply. His movements were slow, his gaze intent on me while Syn worked my pussy, sucking my clit hard until I could take no more, my moaning sounding strange around Gabriel's thick cock as I came, my hips bucking, grinding myself against Syn's tongue.

Gabriel pulled out of my mouth as Syn released me and I slid off the ottoman and onto the floor, breathing hard. I didn't fight them as they rearranged me so that I straddled Syn, taking his cock deep inside me, his length and girth stretching me as he drew me forward to kiss me. Gabriel stood back, watching my face as I moved over Syn, my too tender clit rubbing against Syn's belly with each slow movement.

Syn smiled at me, but when he'd had enough of my soft lovemaking, he turned me over so that I lay on my back. Gabriel took hold of my arms and pulled them up over my head while Syn pushed my legs upward, my knees bent beside my head, my sex spread wide for him. He looked down at it, at me splayed open for him, before returning his gaze to mine as he slid his cock into my pussy. I moaned, trying to free my hands, wanting to wrap them around Syn's neck but wanting Gabriel to hold me down and watch me while his brother fucked my pussy raw. I cried out when I came, feeling Syn release inside me, our gazes locked at this, our most vulnerable moment.

I lay spent when he pulled out of me, but as I looked up into Gabriel's eyes, I knew there was more to come. Syn turned me then so I faced him, my back to Gabriel. Smiling, he positioned me and I knew what he wanted, I knew how Gabriel would have me. Kneeling with the fibers of the carpet digging into my forearms and knees, I presented my bottom to Gabriel, my knees wide, all of me open to him as I hollowed out my back, lifting my hips high. Syn watched while his brother settled behind me, between my legs. Gabriel used his fingers first, stretching and lubricating the tighter passage to ready it for his cock, and I moaned, closing my eyes as he slid first one, then two fingers into me, moving them gently, generously lubricating the inside of my asshole until he deemed me ready to take him.

There was a moment of panic, but it passed as Syn smiled, taking my face in his hands and making me look at him, holding my gaze while his brother penetrated my ass. I panted and gasped while Gabriel took inch after inch. He was patient but unyielding, sliding in and out of me, claiming me while he held me tightly by the hips, and when he settled deep inside me, he pulled me upright for a moment, holding my back to his front, my ass filled with his thick cock, his hands covering my breasts, pinching my nipples, my entire body pure sensation now as he whispered into my ear.

"You're ours now, Evangeline," he said, moving a little inside me, kissing the side of my mouth when I turned my face to his.

"Down," Syn said, taking my hands. "Down on all fours for my brother to fuck you now."

I obeyed, allowing him to position me while Gabriel gripped my hips hard, spreading my bottom wide. I glimpsed over my shoulder to find him watching as he pulled slowly out then pushed into me hard, forcing a cry from my lips, his eyes on my ass as he fucked me, his thrusts coming harder and harder. Syn's gentle hand in my hair was a contrast to Gabriel's hard fucking, and he turned me back to him, a smile on his face before he leaned in to kiss me once more. Gabriel claimed my ass then, and I felt myself wholly and completely theirs. I belonged to them — and they belonged to me.

Gabriel thrust harder, his cock thickening inside me, his fingers closing around my clit, forcing yet another orgasm from me before he came with a rumbling noise from deep within his chest, coming inside me, filling me.

WE ATE ONE OF CAROLINE'S MEALS THAT NIGHT, EACH OF US with a hearty appetite. I felt like a glutton but I was so happy, so very happy. That night we slept together, Gabriel and Syn cocooning me between them, and I knew this was where I belonged, where I was destined to be, safe between them, shared by them, loved by them as I lay there, deep into the night, looking at each of them in turn. My heart felt so full, like nothing I'd ever felt before, a love like I'd never imagined possible.

And for the first time in my life, I was whole.

The End

THANK YOU

Thanks for reading *Theirs To Take!* I hope you enjoyed the book. If you'd consider leaving a review at the store where you purchased this book, I would be so very grateful.

Keep reading for a sample from *Taken!*

Click here to sign up for my newsletter to receive new release news and updates!

Like my FB Author Page to keep updated on news and giveaways!

I have a FB Fan Group where I share exclusive teasers, giveaways and just fun stuff. It's called The Knight Spot. I'd love for you to join us! Just click here!

EXCERPT FROM TAKEN

Helena

I'm the oldest of the Willow quadruplets. Four girls. Always girls. Every single quadruplet birth, generation after generation, it's always girls.

This generation's crop yielded the usual, but instead of four perfect, beautiful dolls, there were three.

And me.

And today, our twenty-first birthday, is the day of harvesting.

That's the Scafoni family's choice of words, not ours. At least not mine. My parents seem much more comfortable with it than my sisters and I do, though.

Harvesting is always on the twenty-first birthday of the quads. I don't know if it's written in stone somewhere or what, but it's what I know and what has been on the back of my mind since I learned our history five years ago.

There's an expression: *those who cannot remember the past are condemned to repeat it.* Well, that's bullshit, because we Willows know well our past and look at us now.

The same blocks that have been used for centuries standing in the old library, their surfaces softened by the feet of every other Willow Girl who stood on the same stumps of wood, and all I can think when I see them, the four lined up like they are, is how archaic this is, how fucking unreal. How they can't do this to us.

Yet, here we are.

And they are doing this to us.

But it's not *us*, really.

My shift is marked.

I'm *unclean*.

So it's really my sisters.

Sometimes I'm not sure who I hate more, my own family for allowing this insanity generation after generation, or the Scafoni monsters for demanding the sacrifice.

"It's time," my father says. His voice is grave.

He's aged these last few months. I wonder if that's remorse because it certainly isn't backbone.

I heard he and my mother argue once, exactly once, and then it was over.

He simply accepted it.

Accepted that tonight, his daughters will be made to stand on those horrible blocks while a Scafoni bastard looks us over, prods and pokes us, maybe checks our teeth like you would a horse, before making his choice. Before taking one of my sisters as his for the next three years of her life.

I'm not naive enough to be unsure what that will mean exactly. Maybe my sisters are, but not me.

"Up on the block. Now, Helena."

I look at my sisters who already stand so meekly on their appointed stumps. They're all paler than usual tonight and I swear I can hear their hearts pounding in fear of what's to come.

When I don't move right away, my father painfully takes my arm and lifts me up onto my block and all I can think, the one thing that gives me the slightest hope, is that if Sebastian Scafoni chooses me, I will find some way to end this. I won't condemn my daughters to this fate. My nieces. My granddaughters.

But he won't choose me, and I think that's why my parents are angrier than usual with me.

See, I'm the ugly duckling. At least I'd be considered ugly standing next to my sisters.

And the fact that I'm unclean—not a virgin—means I won't be taken.

The Scafoni bastard will choose one of their precious golden daughters instead.

Golden, to my dark. Golden—quite literally. Sparkling almost, my sisters.

I glance at them as my father attaches the iron shackle to my ankle. He doesn't do this to any of them. They'll do as they're told, even as their gazes bounce from the closed twelve-foot doors to me and back again and again and again.

But I have no protection to offer. Not tonight. Not on this one.

The backs of my eyes burn with tears I refuse to shed.

"How can you do this? How can you allow it?" I ask for the hundredth time. I'm talking to my mother while my father clasps the restraints on my wrists, making sure I won't attack the monsters.

"Better gag her, too."

It's my mother's response to my question and, a moment later, my father does as he's told and ensures my silence.

I hate my mother more, I think. She's a Willow quadruplet. She witnessed a harvesting herself. Witnessed the result of this cruel tradition.

Tradition.

A tradition of kidnapping.

Of breaking.

Of destroying.

I look to my sisters again. Three almost carbon copies of each other, with long blonde hair curling around their shoulders, flowing down their backs, their blue eyes wide with fear.

Well, except in Julia's case.

She's different than the others. She's more…eager. But I don't think she has a clue what they'll do to her.

Me, no one would guess I came from the same batch.

Opposite their gold, my hair is so dark a black, it appears almost blue, with one single, wide streak of silver to relieve the stark shade, a flaw I was born with. And contrasting their cornflower-blue eyes, mine are a midnight sky; there too, the only relief the silver specks that dot them.

They look like my mother. Like perfect dolls.

I look like my great-aunt, also named Helena, down to the silver streak I refuse to dye. She's in her nineties now. I wonder if they had to lock her in her room and steal her wheelchair, so she wouldn't interfere in the ceremony.

Aunt Helena was the chosen girl of her generation. She knows what's in store for us better than anyone.

"They're coming," my mother says.

She has super hearing, I swear, but then, a moment later, I hear them too.

A door slams beyond the library, and the draft blows out a dozen of the thousand candles that light the huge room.

A maid rushes to relight them. No electricity. Tradition, I guess.

If I were Sebastian Scafoni, I'd want to get a good look at the prize I'd be fucking for the next year. And I have no doubt there will be fucking, because what else can break a girl so completely but taking that of all things?

And it's not just the one year. No. We're given for three years. One year for each brother. Oldest to youngest. It used to be four, but now, it's three.

I would pinch my arm to be sure I'm really standing here, that I'm not dreaming, but my hands are bound behind my back, and I can't.

This can't be fucking real. It can't be legal.

And yet here we are, the four of us, naked beneath our translucent, rotting sheaths—I swear I smell the decay on them—standing on our designated blocks, teetering on them. I guess the Willows of the past had smaller feet. And I admit, as I hear their heavy, confident footfalls approaching the ancient wooden doors of the library, I am afraid.

I'm fucking terrified.

Available now!

ALSO BY NATASHA KNIGHT

Collateral Damage Duet

Collateral: an Arranged Marriage Mafia Romance

Damage: an Arranged Marriage Mafia Romance

Dark Legacy Trilogy

Taken (Dark Legacy, Book 1)

Torn (Dark Legacy, Book 2)

Twisted (Dark Legacy, Book 3)

MacLeod Brothers

Devil's Bargain

Benedetti Mafia World

Salvatore: a Dark Mafia Romance

Dominic: a Dark Mafia Romance

Sergio: a Dark Mafia Romance

The Benedetti Brothers Box Set (Contains Salvatore, Dominic and Sergio)

Killian: a Dark Mafia Romance

Giovanni: a Dark Mafia Romance

Die Benedetto Brüder

Salvatore: Die Benedetto Brüder

Domenico: Die Benedetto Brüder

Killian: Die Benedetto Mafia

Giovanni: Die Benedetto Mafia

The Amado Brothers

Dishonorable

Disgraced

Unhinged

Standalone Dark Romance

Deviant

Beautiful Liar

Retribution

Theirs To Take

Captive, Mine

Alpha

Given to the Savage

Taken by the Beast

Claimed by the Beast

Captive's Desire

Protective Custody

Amy's Strict Doctor

Taming Emma

Taming Megan

Taming Naia

Reclaiming Sophie

The Firefighter's Girl

Dangerous Defiance

Her Rogue Knight

Taught To Kneel

Tamed: the Roark Brothers Trilogy

ABOUT THE AUTHOR

USA Today bestselling author of contemporary romance, Natasha Knight specializes in dark, tortured heroes. Happily-Ever-Afters are guaranteed, but she likes to put her characters through hell to get them there. She's evil like that.

www.natasha-knight.com
natasha-knight@outlook.com